Trickster Jack

E. Reid Gilbert

Trickster Jack

Copyright © 2009 E. Reid Gilbert. All rights reserved. No part of this book may be reproduced or retransmitted in any form or by any means without the written permission of the publisher.

Cover design by Susan Wenger.
Interior illustrations by Garrett Clark.

Published by Wheatmark®
610 East Delano Street, Suite 104
Tucson, Arizona 85705 U.S.A.
www.wheatmark.com

Publisher's Cataloging-In-Publication Data
(Prepared by The Donohue Group, Inc.)

Gilbert, E. Reid.   Trickster Jack / E. Reid Gilbert ; [illustrations by Garrett Clark].
   p. : ill. ; cm.
 ISBN: 978-1-60494-237-8
1. Tricksters—Fiction. 2. Tales—Appalachian Region. 3. Proverbs—Appalachian Region. 4. Folklore—Appalachian Region. I. Clark, Garrett. II. Title.

GR108.15 .G55 2009
398.22   2008943440

This book is dedicated to my three daughters, Tari, Adrienne, and Karen, all of whom endured many hours of stories, songs, and ol'-time sayin's, with the hope that they will share those memories and these tales with my grandchildren, Alexis, Clayton, Sam, Priya, Theo, and Maia.

Contents

Tricksters vii
Jack an' the Candlestick 1
Little Jack Horner 11
Jack Plays Mother Goose 21
Jack's Childhood Sweetheart 35
Jack's New Wagon 45
Jack's End of a Romance 53
A Penny Saved 61
Jack's Diet 77
Ol' Jack 87
Ol' Jack's Indoor-Outhouse 93
The Jack Game 101

Tricksters
or, The Globalization of Foolery

Having grown up in the southern Appalachian Mountains under the storytelling tutelage of Richard Chase, the author of *Jack Tales* and *Grandfather Tales*, I have come to appreciate the mischief maker Jack. Later I was introduced to cunning Ananzi of Africa, lawbreaker Sri Thanonchai of Thailand, wily Coyote of Native American stories, boasting Karagoz of Turkey, bumbling Hanswurst of Germany, and scheming Harlequin of Italy. I even spent time in England tracking down Little Devil Doubt of the ancient mummers' plays. It seems that every culture has its own trickster character, differing only in part from the imps of other cultures.

It is obvious that Shakespeare was aware of these traditional characters, particularly for the character of the Fool in *King Lear*. Even though the Fool played tricks and teased everyone, including Lear, he was the only one who could survive telling the truth to the king. Perhaps only through tomfoolery do we unearth the truth of the human condition and relationships.

Although each of these tricksters is unique, they all exhibit some similar traits such as laziness, gluttony, boastfulness, and, of course, cleverness. They also come from a lower social class and often act contrary to the limits of the law and beyond the bounds of moral codes. They are certainly not role models, and yet each is endearing to admirers who can relate to his peasant roots as he challenges authoritative persons and conventions.

Each is usually a master linguist in whatever culture he appears, using an accepted idiom but interpreting it literally, or using language in such a way as to confuse or deliberately mislead his opponents. Sri Thanonchai uses verbal trickery to get a second wife, while Jack flouts English grammar rules against double negatives when he declares quite determinedly with a quintuple negative: "I don't never take nothin' off nobody, nohow." When he is subsequently corrected by his teacher, who also states that inversely a double affirmative can never become a negative, Jack answers with a sarcastic, "Yeah, right!" positively proving his teacher negative. The reader can begin to sympathize with any verbal opponent of Jack or his fellow tricksters.

One of the appealing facets of the trickster figure is that he seems to have absolute freedom to make whatever choice he wishes, and although his choices are always in his self-interest he never seems to be self-centered or egotistical. He invites us with his sense of playful freedom into the realm of humor, and recent medical research has confirmed the healing power of humor. Also, ironically, Jack and his compatriot tricksters exhibit faith in the ultimate moral structure of the universe, which can withstand their onslaughts of foolishness and rascality.

This excursive interest of mine has not been confined to academic and scholarly research. Much of my information and inspiration have come from neighbors and family members.

Tricksters

So, with these globalized tricksters in mind and my own Great-uncle Sammy Jane as inspiration, I dare to turn Jack, the Appalachian trickster, loose on a question that has bedeviled many a folk for a long time: where did all those nursery rhymes and old-timey sayings originate, and under what conditions?

Now, Jack was known far and wide for his tricks and rascally jokes. Everybody around had either been the butt of one of his practical jokes or knew someone who had come out on the short end of the stick in some kind of dealings with him.

Yet, for all his energy in foolishness he was uncommonly lazy. His own grandma, not wanting to own up to his laziness, said he was "just born tired and never got rested up."

He was also a glutton and never seemed to gain any weight. His uncle Moyer said that he ate so much that it "tired him out just carrying it aroun'," and the exercise of it kept him as skinny as a rail.

It seemed that no matter what happened to him or anybody around him, Jack would have something to say about it, making up a little saying like, "Don't count your chickens before they're hatched." Some of the sayings are still around today, although, over time, some of them have been changed or forgotten.

So we'll just take a look at how Jack had a hand in coming up with some of those old rhymes and sayings.

Jack an' the Candlestick

You probably already heard about Jack—most folks either know somethin' on him or at least've heard uv some uv his trickery ways, the scrapes an' rapscallion situations he got hisself into an' usually out uv. He was a born natural fer cookin' up some kind uv mischief—jest fer the devilment uv it—or jumpin' into somethin' when he shoulda been payin' more 'tention.

In fact, hit was someone what tole him thet he shoulda been lookin' closter—probably somethin' his daddy woulda said, 'cause he was allus tryin' to correck Jack. Well, Jack turned thet admonition into the ol'-time sayin' "Look afore you leap."

Now, Jack lived quite some time ago, but he was so well known thet lots uv sayin's can be traced back to some kinda foolery he got hisself into. This here story will be a kinda English lesson, though I hate to own up to it. You see, Jack actually invented some uv the words in our language, which you'll find out 'bout.

Even though Jack's time uv life was a long time ago, some uv his remainin' family lived acrost a couple uv ridges from one uv my cousins, Lige Bowen, an' hit was him what tole me on Jack so many times.

Now, I'll have to be straight with you; I cain't rightly say thet I believed all them things thet wuz tole on Jack fer a couple uv reasons: in the first place Lige was the outlandishest hand to add a little somethin' extra to a pot even if hit was already a-boilin' (he was awful bad to drink, don't you know), an' in the second place I couldn't hardly believe thet Jack or nobody else coulda gotten hisself into half those scrapes reported on 'im an' come out alive or without landin' up in jail someplace.

Now this here was one special time when there was quite a bit uv talk about the doctor's daughter. Oh, there weren't anythin' particular wrong with her. Hit was jest thet her circumstances were a little bit peculiar, an' you know how thet goes when things are not right on track, so to speak—well, folks would begin to talk. An' the honest fact was thet the girl was already sixteen, wadn't married, an' hadn't even begun to talk with any uv the boys in the neighborhood, nur outside, so far as anybody knew.

She jest didn't seem to be innerested, an' what's more the local boys didn't seem to be innerested in her. Now this was most peculiar, particularly when hit comes to Jack, 'cause ever'body commented on how he'd pay real close 'tention to a pretty face an' carry on 'bout thet with his brothers, Will an' Tom. An' she was a pretty thing. All the boys noticed Jack's disint'rest an' 'fronted him 'bout it. He jest said, "A feller jest has to have a little show fer him to go on an' make a fool uv his own self. I jest cain't tell whether she's innerested in anythin'. She don't laugh, she don't cry, she don't frown, she don't even sigh." The boys all laughed at thet little poem an' opinioned thet when she was off to school yonder, things must've been so tarnashously excitin' thet nothin' here back home could ever measure up.

Jack an' the Candlestick

An' they were exactly right. She was jest teetotally bored with the old hometown an' even more so with the old hometown boys. Now her father, the doctor, suspicioned thet she might have some kinda ailment, what he called psychosomethin' or 'nother. But he decided thet afore he'd send her back to the big city to see a mind specialist, he'd try somethin'—a kind uv experiment, don't you know—an' thet's what he done.

He let hit out thet any boy or man what could get her to break her morbid silence with a tear, a laugh, an applause, or even a smile ... why then he'd hire the lucky fellow to be foreman uv his sawmill an' might even talk with the boy 'bout marryin' his daughter—that is if she's innerested. An' why wouldn't she be innerested; she surely wadn't innerested in anythin' else.

Jack nur none uv his brothers was married, an' all uv 'em would really 'preciate a steady job, especially as foreman uv the sawmill; why then the rest uv the neighbor folks would really look up to them. I mean what with the good wages an' bein' able to hire an' fire anyone you pleased—that would be an uncommonly favorable prestige. Any one uv the three boys would welcome a good wife, particularly the daughter uv the doctor.

Well now, most uv the other men an' boys had tried their hand at one fool thing or 'nother. But thet pore girl jest looked at each one uv their efforts with a blank look on her face—not even an expression uv disgust or exasperation.

So Jack an' his brothers, Will an' Tom, thought they'd give the matter a try. Hit hadn't been long afore thet they'd all gone into town when a circus was performin' there, an' they figgered thet since they'd seen so many foreign things an' excitin' acts there thet Lorene—that was the doctor's daughter's name—that Lorene might take notice uv somethin' like thet. So they begun to practice some uv those circus acts afore they'd actually perform them in public fer sech grand prizes.

Now Will, bein' the oldest uv the brothers, was the first to try. He had been particularly mindful uv the tightwire act, so he allowed as how he would use the top rail uv the rail fence in place uv a tightwire. Jack cautioned him about the pig's slop trough bein' next to the fence. Will didn't pay him no nevermind; after all, he was the oldest an' ever'body knows the older brother never likes to take advice from a younger brother. Will was bound an' determined to do things his own way, so thet's what he done.

Unfortunately, he hadn't reckoned on thet top rail bein' a little loose, an' by the time he had took his second step out onto thet rail, hit squiggled jest a little under his feet; but hit was jest enough to make him lose his balance an' head foremost he toppled right over into thet hog trough an' hit full uv kitchen scraps an' hog slop. Jack kinda murmured under his breath—his advice havin' been ignored—"Pride goeth afore a fall." As I've already mentioned, Jack was noted fer startin' a lot uv them old-time sayin's.

Well, when Will sat up with all thet filthy stuff all over him an' a cabbage leaf where his hat oughta uv been, ever'body busted out laughin'. Some laughed so hard they almost fell off their own selves from where they'd been awatchin' the show.

But not Lorene; she jest sat there. She almost twinged a look uv disgust but hit didn't register enough on her face fer her daddy to notice any real change in her countenance.

Jack tole Will thet was what he got fer not movin' the hog trough an' bein' so "pigheaded." Thet's when Jack made up thet word, "pigheaded," 'cause Will's head was filled with pig slop. Jack also called Will "will-full," him insistin' on havin' his own way an' not takin' good advice. Thet's where the English vocabulary got the word "willful," which Jack made up an' basically means insistin' on havin' yore own way. In the end the hog's feedin' trough was full uv Will, simply because he wouldn't pay no 'tention to some good advice.

Tom was next on the agenda—him bein' the next oldest brother. He had decided to emulate the trapeze artists. He was goin' to swing out uv the barn loft, turn a somerset in the air, an' land in a pile uv corn shucks left over from last night's corn shuckin'. He'd been practicin' real regular an' had gotten pretty good at thet mid-air somerset. But jest afore the performance, while still in the barn loft an' unbeknownst to anybody—even Will an' Jack—he decided he'd better have a costume like the circus performers. So he stripped off his shirt an' overhauls down to his skivvies (his underwear) 'cause to the best uv his recollection the circus folks had performed in their long-johns (winter underwear).

But don't you know, jest as he was aswingin' out uv the barn loft, his skivvies caught on a nail stickin' out there, an' when he swung on out his skivvies didn't—they stayed hangin' on thet obtrusive nail. Tom was so surprised by this unfortunate turn uv events thet he fergot to do the somerset; in fact he even fergot to let go uv the rope an' jest hung out there in all his glory over thet pile uv corn shucks, naked as a jaybird.

When he finally come to hisself he figgered he'd better let go uv the rope an' go ahead an' land in the corn shucks, instead uv hangin' out there, so to speak, fer the whole wide world to ogle. So he let go uv the rope an' stayed half hidden in the corn shucks 'til Jack brung him his overhauls. He really didn't need his skivvies anyway. Now hit was jest foolishness what made him strip down to his skivvies thetaway, an' Jack called hit "tomfoolery." Thet's how we come by thet word, "tomfoolery," which simply means the foolishness uv Tom.

TRICKSTER JACK

Now, o' course this caused a good deal uv snickerin', but not from Lorene. She jest turned her head—maybe to conceal a slight smirk on her face. But her daddy didn't take no notice uv even thet trace uv an almost changed expression.

Now, hit was time fer Jack, an' he didn't waste no time atall but started right into his act, which was a jugglin' routine inspired from what he had seen at the circus. Though the circus clowns juggled balls an' bowlin' pins, Jack had planned somethin' a little different. Many times he had swung a bucket full uv milk over his head while headin' back to the house after milkin' time an' afore hit was strained an' put in the spring house fer coolin'. He had also perfected this little feat with buckets uv water from the spring—sometimes two at a time.

What he would do was to swing the full bucket over his head, an' as long as he kept hit goin' fast enough, the liquid—whatever hit was—wouldn't spill out even when hit was upside down. He hadn't made more than a couple uv mistakes with this trick; thet would be when he become uncertain an' slowed down when the bucket was over his head—that'd been rather disastrous. But hit would mean a good wrenchin' bath whether hit was Saturday or not.

He had developed this little game 'cause he would get bored jest carryin' a bucket uv water or milk, an' he was allus conductin' an experiment uv one sort or 'nother.

'Cause he was so familiar with this little trick, he had all the confidence in the world hit would go jest right. Well you know, he taken a bucket full uv milk an', holdin' on to the bale uv the bucket he started swingin' hit faster an' faster an' higher an' higher.

Then jest to check on the situation, he decided to look over to

6

thet girl to see what kind uv impression he was makin'; but, don't you know, thet little tactic uv his hesitated him jest enough fer thet bucket uv milk to spill its entire contents right over his head.

He begun spittin' an' sputterin', an' ever'body wuz gettin' the biggest kick out uv Jack doin' this to his own self, 'cause they allus seen him comin' out on the long end uv the stick whenever he was in any kind uv contentious predicament. But then they reckoned he'd done this on purpose to get some kind uv rise out uv Lorene. He sure wadn't 'bout to let on thet he hadn't deliberately intended to do exactly what they seen him do. Thet's when he started thet old-time sayin', "No use cryin' over spilt milk."

Well, ever'one looked over at the doctor's daughter, an' she wadn't sayin' nothin' an' wadn't doin' a thing 'cept coverin' her mouth with a little hankie to catch a sneeze. Actually she had used the handkerchief to conceal a little smile thet was about to form on her face. She was beginnin' to take a likin' to this fellow Jack, but she wadn't 'bout to let on thet she was becomin' innerested in him. She was enjoyin' the 'tention she was gettin' from her daddy an' ever'one else.

Now, hit looked like all the boys had failed at gettin' Lorene to respond to any uv their courtin' shenanigans, but Jack an' his brothers asked the doctor if they could try one more time as a team—a kind uv family act, don't you know. The good doctor thought on thet a minute an' concluded thet hit was fair enough since there didn't seem to be any more candidates on hand. He figured he'd try 'most anythin' to avoid sendin' Lorene off to see the mind doctor in the city.

So real quick-like the brothers begun to form a human pyramid with Will on the bottom—him bein' the oldest—and then with Tom crawlin' up onto his shoulders. Lastly, Jack clumb up over

Will to Tom's shoulders, an' jest as Jack was 'bout to do a handstand on top uv Tom's head, thet girl looked as though she was about to applaud.

The crowd gasped loud enough fer the boys to hear, an' when they looked over her way they lost their balance an' fell on top uv each other in a tangled heap.

Now instead uv clappin' as she was wont to do, thet girl laughed right out loud jest like hit wuz a ever'day thing fer her. The crowd by this time wuz havin' more fun than they would've had at the real circus.

Hit surely looked like the doctor had hisself a sawmill foreman an' possibly a new son-in-law. But now hit was a different problem; the sawmill couldn't have three foremen an' Lorene couldn't have three husbands—not legally anyway. So what to do?

Well the doctor asked Lorene if she wanted to make a choice uv one uv the three brothers; wuz she maybe more partial to one than the others? She was kinda takin' a shine to Jack, but she was also beginnin' to have sech fun with all this nonsense—even more fun than she'd had in the big city—so she said thet the final contenders oughta have a little contest 'twixt the three uv them to declare a final winner.

That's what they done: Jack an' Will an' Tom had to see which one could run through the bull lot without the bull gorin' 'em to death, then run past the mean wolfhound tied in the doctor's backyard without gettin' bitten. The first one to get past or through those obstacles wuz to come an' jump over a lighted candlestick without gettin' burnt, an' thet would be a signal thet he would be the one wantin' to marry her.

Well those three brothers took off from the startin' point like the spring on a rabbit trap. When they jumped almost at the same

Jack an' the Candlestick

time into thet bull pen thet girl said to herself, "Now Jack, please be nimble aroun' Ol' Bayllis Bull." An' sure 'nough Jack jest fairly skipped aroun' thet feller, an' by the time thet brute realized what was goin' on he made up his mind to put a stop to this foolishness.

Well, he made right fer Jack, but Jack'd already cleared the fence. Will was right handy nearby so the old bull was able to hook one uv Will's overhaul suspenders with his horn, but Will was able to jerk loose. While Ol' Bayliss was messin' with Will, why Tom had run past an' was over the fence.

Now hit was time fer Chester, the wolfhound, to participate in the game. He was half asleep under the Chinaberry tree. As Jack approached cautiously in high hopes thet Chester would keep on sleepin', he made up in his own mind the sayin' "Better let sleepin' dogs lie." Thet old dog did open one eye an' then the other.

When Lorene seen both those eyes open, she said under her breath, "Jack you better be quick." an' sure enough almost as if he'd heard her say hit, Jack liked to have jumped out uv his skin jest when the dog growled somethin' fierce, jumpin' to the end uv his chain, barely missin' Jack. While Chester was beratin' hisself fer missin' Jack, Will had whizzed past, but thet wolfhound was in time to take a big patch right out uv the seat uv Tom's overhauls, an' him already havin' lost his skivvies.

By now all three boys wuz headin' twarge thet candle in front uv Lorene almost in a dead heat. But Will was havin' to hold up his overhauls 'cause uv his broken galluses, an' Tom was holdin' his hands over the bare spot where the dog had took a chunk out uv the seat uv his britches.

Lorene was laughin' so hard thet she could hardly maintain her neutrality. She was hopin' thet in spite of hit all thet Jack would get there first, so she muttered, "Jack jump over this candlestick."

TRICKSTER JACK

That's exactly what Jack done. Then she said right out loud what she'd been sayin' to herself an' she didn't care who heard it, "Jack be nimble, Jack be quick." An' she announced to her daddy, "See, Jack jumped over the candlestick." Thet's another uv those old-time sayin's Jack had a hand in.

So Jack married Lorene an' become foreman uv the sawmill. He hired Tom to be the sawyer an' Will to be payroll clerk.

After the dust had settled from all the goin's-on, Jack sat in his big rockin' chair on the front porch an' rared back an' said, "Well, all's well what ends well."

You know over in Old England where the king lives—not in New England where the shanty Irish Kennedys live—a writer fellow heard about thet sayin', an' they say he wrote a whole play-party thing an' named hit "All's Well Thet Ends Well."

Little Jack Horner

What I'm agonna tell you now 'bout Jack was when he was jest a little feller. All uv a sudden, one day, he decided he'd try schoolin'. He'd heard Will an' Tom an' older young'uns talk about the schoolhouse, the teacher, the school programs, an' so on. Some uv the things he heard were a little scary an' some were downright excitin'.

He had already learned most uv the alphabet from his brothers' textbooks, but he got a bit mixed up when they had taught him how to spell Mississippi. Actually, he was at first confused about the word, as he thought hit meant his neighbor, whose nickname was Sis an' had married Howard Sippy. A'course, Jack would allus address older folks with either Miss, Mrs., or Mr. So a'course he thought her full name was Missus Sis Sippy, an' when he heard the name uv the state uv Mississippi, he thought they had named a state after his neighbor.

Well, his brothers helped him to remember the spellin' uv the state with *M-I- crookedletter-crookedletter-I-crookedletter-crookedlet-*

Little Jack Horner

ter-I-humpback- humpback-I. After thet he got the *Ms* an' *Is* jest fine but an S was to him a crooked letter an' a P was a humpback.

Even with this miseducation, he thought he'd try schoolin' anyways, even though he'd had warnin's about the dangers uv becomin' a educated fool. He wadn't sure what thet meant, but he assured hisself he wouldn't fall into thet awesome pit.

Well, he was tol'ably good at school an' seemed to get along fine with ever'body, includin' Miss Harris, the teacher, who took a likin' to him. She could be kinda strict sometime, but she was awful impressed with Jack an' his quick-wittedness. He was also good in spellin' an' had already fergot thet stuff about a S bein' a crooked letter an' a P bein' a humpback, but he still liked to spell, usin' unusual ways to name the letters.

I should mention thet Jack was a shirt-tail boy til he went off to school. What a shirt-tail boy means is thet little boys, after they had outgrown their dydies, in the summertime jest wore a long-tail shirt, kinda like a dress, but without britches or overhauls. Hit was real convenient, 'cause the little feller wouldn't be encumbered with pant legs flappin' aroun' his legs. The shirt-tail was no longer than necessary, but hit did cover necessary.

Some little boys, Jack bein' one uv 'em, was so attached to thet particular fashion uv clothin' thet they put off the pant-wearin' habit jest as long as possible. In fact, Jack had kept postponin' wearin' britches so long thet Will an' Tom called him Shirt-tail Jack.

Now, one day the teacher called on Jack's class to spell "chicken," but they couldn't spell hit until hit was time fer Shirt-tail Jack to spell. He approached the task in his own particular way. The rest uv the class got a big kick out uv his spellin' it, an' one uv the older girls made up a poem about it:

TRICKSTER JACK

There was a mountain schoolhouse
Across the wagon track.
There was a country schoolboy
By the name of Shirt-tail Jack.
Now when it come to spelling
He could always bring words fast.
He was the only learned scholar
Who could stand down his own class.
Now one day the teacher called on his class
To spell a kind of bird;
That sort of bird was chicken,
But they could not spell that word.
So then they called on Shirt-tail Jack
To spell that word for them,
He did not hesitate one bit,
But this is the way he begun;
"Oh, C is the way to begin;
H is the next letter then;
I, that is the third;
C is the fillin' of the bird;
K is near the end;
E is next to the end;
C-H-I-C-K-E-N
That is the way you spell 'chicken.'"

The very next summer when the schoolhouse was turned over to the ol' Baptist preacher fer music school, why, he let thet girl turn the poem into a little song which all the chil'ren learned. Thet was probably the first sayin' or song or nursery rhyme what Jack come up with, or at any rate was made up about him.

Though Jack was beginnin' to be noticed fer his school smarts, hit didn't take him long to get into some kinda mischief. Now because the teacher was kinda partial to Jack, she didn't take too much notice to some uv the little mishaps what started happenin' aroun' the school an' what some uv the chil'ren laid off on Jack.

Little Jack Horner

She hadn't asked him directly, an' he wadn't about to tell. Thet was where the "Don't ask, don't tell" sayin' got started.

Now hit was a honor fer the teacher to appoint one uv the chil'ren to help with a schoolhouse chore like wipin' the blackboard or sweepin' the floor or gettin' in the stove wood. But what Jack wanted to do in the worst kind uv way was to take the water bucket to the spring an' get drinkin' water fer all uv the chil'ren.

The teacher usually asked one uv the older boys to do this, 'cause the wooden bucket full uv water would be kinda heavy. But Jack kept volunteerin', so to speak, so she assigned him the task pretty soon one mornin' after the school bell had summoned the chil'ren into the schoolhouse fer their lessons.

So Jack took off down the hill twarge the spring with thet big bucket a-bouncin' against his heels every step he took, but he didn't pay no nevermind, 'cause he figgered he was growin' up, havin' been designated the water boy fer the day. Also he was gettin' out uv some long division arithmetic, what he already knew.

When he got down to the spring he jest couldn't resist takin' off at least one shoe to dip his big toe into the branch water right below the spring, even though hit was in December right after Christmas.

When he stuck thet bare foot into the icy branch water, he yelled an' jumped back, steppin' with his bare foot on a brier. Well, he set down on a big rock right then an' there above the spring house an' tried his darndest to dig thet brier out with his jackknife, which had been named "Jackknife" after him because he liked his foldin'-up knife so well—they also named hit after Jack, 'cause, jest like Jack hit was useless when left to itself, but could do a lot uv good or damage with a strong hand either pushin' or pullin' hit. Thet brier was jest as stubborn as Jack an' refused to budge from its hidin' place there in the sole uv Jack's foot.

So he put his shoe back on an' hobbled over to the spring to fill up the bucket, but the bucket, when hit was filled, was so heavy hit nearly pulled him headforem'st over into the spring. He allowed thet wouldn't do atall so he sloshed some water outta the bucket so's hit wouldn't be so heavy fer him.

Then he got to thinkin' about thet brier in his foot an' how he had tried so hard to gouge hit out with his jackknife. Now, thet brier give him a idee; an' you know he was allus, even then, schemin' up some trick or 'nother. Hit was then he made up the sayin' "Misery loves company," as he started figurin', with the brier as inspiration, some way to share his misery.

Right there directly above the footpath was a thornapple tree with long thorns more'n two inches long. He cut one uv the longest thorns, an' after takin' his right brogan off, he stuck thet thorn out the toe end uv his shoe.

Well now, he pulled thet bucket nearly full uv water behind him all the way up the hill with the water sloshin' all over the legs uv his britches an' hit bein' miserable cold winter like hit was. By the time he got back he was so tarnashusly miserable with the brier in his foot an' his wet overalls thet he looked like he was gonna cry, an' ever'body took pity on him.

The teacher let him set fer awhile right next to the wood stove near where the big girls sat. Although he did like the 'tention he was gettin', he had kinda changed his mind about the honorable privilege uv gettin' to go to the spring fer drinkin' water, particular considerin' the size uv the wooden bucket an' hits weight when hit was most nearly full uv water.

While settin' next to the stove, still feelin' the pain of thet brier, he took off thet shoe an' pretty soon was able to pull hit out an' throw hit over in the wood box. Right then he come up with thet old riddle, which chil'ren still enjoy to this day:

I went to the woods to get it.
The more I looked fer it the more I hated it.
When I couldn't find it I brought it home.
When I did find it I threw it away.
What was it?

Jack's answer, a'course was "a brier."

Now while Jack's shoe was off, hit come to him what was the destiny-mission of that thornapple tree thorn. When he went back to his seat after dryin' off, he settled down real quiet-like with his book open an' pretendin' to read. Instead uv studyin' his lesson, he was studyin' Pete Dalton settin' right in front uv him, an' when Pete quit squirmin' aroun' in his seat, why Jack real slow-like stuck the toe uv his brogan with the thorn out the front up behind Pete's seat. Then when ever'body was payin' 'tention to the teacher, Jack jabbed thet thorn into Pete's behind. When Pete yelled like a kicked pup, the teacher asked, "What's the matter, Pete?" but he didn't let on atall what had happened.

When the teacher wadn't lookin', Pete turned aroun' an' glowered at Jack. "I vow an' declare I'm agonna get even with you." Then when Jack started thet thorny foot back up twarge Pete's seat agin the teacher seen hit a-happenin'. She caught him red-handed, so to speak, or at least thorn-footed. She called Jack up to her desk an' gave him a dunce cap, which she kept handy fer jest sech occasions. "Now you put this on an' go sit on the stool in the corner." This ritual was designated fer errant scholars.

As hit was now nearly dinnertime, Jack asked if he could fetch his dinner pail. She said thet hit would be alright, as she was still in the Christmas spirit. Jack had brought some uv his mamma's Christmas pie. While his back was turned to the class he got to foolin' aroun' an' messin' aroun' with thet pie. Then unthoughtedly, so to speak, he blurted right out, "I am a good boy," 'cause he'd been studyin' on how ever'body kept throwin' off on him bein' mischievous an' sech a bad boy.

The teacher an' all the chil'ren started lookin' at 'im an' laughin', 'cause he had a plum on the end uv his thumb an' plum pie fillin' smeared all aroun' his mouth. Hit was then thet Pete Dalton thought he'd squar things off with Jack by writin' a silly poem about him. Although Horner wadn't Jack's last name, Pete had to find a word to rhyme with corner. So he wrote:

> Little Jack Horner
> Sat in a corner,
> Eating his Christmas pie.
> He stuck in his thumb
> And pulled out a plum
> And said, "What a good boy am I!"

Now when Miss Harris saw Pete writin' somethin' down on his tablet, she suspicioned thet he might be writin' a love note to Betsy Bowman, who ever'body knew he'd been talkin' to uv late. So the teacher, jest to teach a lesson to Pete, had him write his supposed love note on the blackboard in order to humiliate him an' Betsy to not anymore be writin' an' passin' love notes in school.

All the pupils were holdin' their breath in anticipation uv readin' a public juicy love note what they knew Pete was capable uv writin'. When he wrote out the first line "Little Jack Horner" they noticed this wadn't what they wuz expectin', an' they begun to snicker. By time he wrote out the second line "Sat in a corner" they were all pointin' at Jack an' laughin' an' havin' a hoot uv a good time at Jack's expense, an' instead uv laughin' at Pete's love note they wuz pokin' fun at Jack's unfortunate circumstance.

Pore Jack was dogged an' bedeviled by thet Little Jack Horner rhyme fer the rest uv his school days, an' if truth be known the rest, uv his natcheral life. But Jack, right then an' there, declared to hisself thet from then on if there was to be any jokes to be played on a'body, why he'd be on the givin' end an' somebody else—it didn't differ who—would be on the receivin' end. Hit was then he made up thet sayin', "Hit's better to give than to receive."

Jack Plays Mother Goose

Ever' summer Jack an' his brothers, Will an' Tom, along with all the other neighbor chil'ren, would go to music school, what was conducted in the old church house not so far from their home. They called hit "music school," but hit allus jest worked on singin' an' didn't teach no musical instruments atall.

There was those folks, mainly men, in the community what did play music on the fiddle, guitar, an' dulcimer an' zither. Some used jest ordinary things to bang away on like spoons an' lard buckets or made bass fiddles out uv a warshtub an' strong cord tied to a stick at one end an' knotted on the other end through a hole in the middle uv the tub. Others might play a juice harp or comb with a piece uv cellophane. Whiskey jugs also—after they was emptied—could be used to blow a bass drone fer all the melodies. A real talented feller might use a fiddle bow on a handsaw.

A few folks—mostly women—played the piano or pump organ, but they was usually too big to carry aroun' like all the other instruments...I meant the piano was too big to lug aroun', not the women...though some uv them wuz considerable sizable their own selves. But I don't wanna lay off on the women folks thetaway.

Twarge the close uv summer when the crops would be laid by but afore the "bringin' in the sheaves" was begun an' the singin' lessons was finished, why, they'd have a big to-do fer the parents an' neighbors to see an' hear how well the chil'ren had all done with their singin' lessons.

A coupla years earlier than what I'm now tellin' you about this particular happenin', the teachers had begun to teach shape-note singin'. Now what this meant was thet when the songwriter would write out the tune on a musical staff, he'd give all the notes a particular shape...a squar, a diamond, a circle, or one uv two different triangle shapes...only five notes on thet music scale. So the singer, oncet he learned the shapes like learnin' the alphabet fer book readin', could then read the music at first sight, what they now call "sight readin'." Nearly all the chil'ren got pretty good at thet sight readin'.

It seemed thet ever'body, whether they had chil'ren in the singin' school or not, would look forward to this little performance, what would come at the end uv dog days. Some got to callin' the performance a "recital," but they won't no call to do thet fer there wadn't no recitin' goin' on, jest the singin', don't you know. But by the folks callin' hit a recital, why, thet give Jack an' the boys a idee what might make the whole affair a little more innerestin' than jest shape note singin'.

Jack at this time musta been 'bout twelve an' his brothers, Will an' Tom, acourse, a little bit older. As a matter a fact, Will an' Tom was gettin' 'most too old to take the summer music school, an' thet mighta sparked a good reason fer doin' somethin' special.

Jack Plays Mother Goose

Jack said thet they wanted to have their own swan song, 'specially when they announced they wanted to do some playactin' animals an' their ways uv doin' things—the noises they made an' the way they moved an' all. Jack surmised thet they wanted to play beautiful swans, an' thet's why he called hit their swan song. Ever' summer since then folks have noted thet when a person is to do their last thing ever, it'd be his "swan song," though hit was Jack what made up thet sayin'.

Ever'body was used to seein' the ol' mummers' plays at Christmastime, an' several uv the boys was in it ever' year when it went from house to house, cavortin' with wooden swords, a hobbyhorse, some singin' an' dancin', an', acourse, beggin' fer soulcakes or some other Christmas goodies. But thet allus happened in the wintertime, an' besides thet they had only boys who'd taken part in it, an' the music school was in the summer an' had both boys an' girls in it.

One uv the things all the chil'ren was fascinated by, uv all the farm animals they knew, was the ol' mamma goose, an' in particular how she would protect her little goslin's even fernenst a ferocious dog or cat. On the other hand, they'd seed a goose do some weird or stupid or even cunnin' things; an' if abody was to do the same sort uv thing, why they'd call him a goose. A'course with all the shenanigans Jack had pulled at one time or 'nother, he'd often been called a goose.

So sure enough, they decided thet they'd do some playactin' about animals, an' the main character was gonna be a mamma goose. As soon as they'd decided thet much, Will an' Tom an' even their cousin, Pete, put forth the notion thet Jack was to play the mamma goose, 'cause he's allus actin' a silly goose anyways.

Well now, Jack put up a real fuss about thet. He didn't like the idee atall, 'cause the mamma goose oughta be played by a girl, but

Tom said, "That don't make no nevermind, 'cause whoever plays the old mamma goose will be covered by a costume an' nobody's likely to know whether it be a boy or a girl." Jack still said he wadn't gonna stand fer it.

Well, Jill, who at thet time was still sweet on Jack an' wanted to play the part her own self, suggested thet they all take a vote on who should be appointed to play the part uv Mamma Goose.

This was about the time there in the ol' country when folks was gettin" tired uv the king or the high sheriff allus appointin' their own man, as well as how a certain thing was gonna be done. So thet was when they decided thet the fairest way to do things was to vote on them, an' if a body was needed fer special work to do, why then ever'body would jest vote, an' thet would be the way hit would be.

A'course, now, thet had been the way things had allus been done in Jack's neighborhood, but hit sometimes seemed thet hit took the rest uv the world a little bit more time to catch up with the way things was done down to home.

So they all voted, an' a'course Jack got a whole lot more votes than Jill. The boys was put up to it jest to have a little more fun with Jack, who'd played too many tricks on them. Jill cried a little when she didn't get but a few votes, an' one uv them a'course was Jack's. He didn't like atall how the 'lection had turned out, but he promised to abide by it an' be the best mamma goose he could be; thet is, if Jill was to be given the part uv the beautiful swan an' have a little dance.

Nobody seemed to object to Jill playin' a swan. Jack had tole her a story about a baby ugly ducklin' what growed up to be a beautiful growed-up swan, an' she liked particular the part about growin' up to be beautiful. So they all agreed to thet, an' Jill felt a whole lot better about thet . . . an' about Jack.

He then whispered to her, "Now, I've got a little secret, an' I ain't gonna tell nobody but you thet there's gonna be some extra excitement when the actual performance is to take place. Hit'll be unbeknownst to ever'body else—but you got to pledge not to tell nobody, nohow."

She promised thet she'd keep the secret, but she wanted to know more about what the secret would actually be. Jack said, "Fer the time bein' we'll both jest have to be content with knowin' there's gonna be a big surprise the night uv the big to-do."

The main reason Jack didn't tell Jill right then an' there about the details uv the big excitement was the fact thet he didn't know fer sure his own self. What he did know was thet he wadn't pleased atall with Will an' Tom an' Cousin Pete puttin' up the other chil'ren to vote fer him to play the mamma goose.

Now one uv them older boys, what was mostly to blame fer Jack gettin' the part uv the mamma goose, said, "If Jill can play a animal what none uv us ain't never seen, I allow hit should be all right fer some uv us to play animals we ain't never seen, 'stead uv some ol' cow or pig or other more usual farm brute." Ever'body seemed to think thet stood to reason.

Well, Will right off sez, "I'm gonna play a big slithery python snake." He started wigglin' his arm twarge the littler ones, makin' out he was gonna swallow them an' causin' them to squeal.

Pete announced, "Well then, I'm gonna be a gorilla." Ever'body started sayin' they'd allus figgered he was a monkey anyways.

Tom said, "Now, I seen this picture uv a kangaroo, an' hit might be fun to hop aroun' like one uv them critters." A kangaroo was a funny animal with a big tail an' a stomach pouch like a mamma possum.

Jack woulda been happy to aplayed any one uv them animals,

but as he'd already agreed to the deal, he didn't say nothin' further.

All the rest uv the chil'ren was to play little goslin's, an' ducks, an' chickens, an' other familiar farm animals. They was to study on them an' how they walked an' sech, an' what kinda sounds they might make fer talkin'.

The chil'ren started in workin' on their parts whenever they wadn't out workin' in the fields or when the practicin' didn't come in the way uv their chores. They, a'course, had to decide what the story was gonna be about an' what the different animals was gonna be sayin' to each other.

They was used to the fightin' in the mummers plays, so they decided thet Mamma Goose was gonna have to fight over her little goslin's, an' when she got killed hit would be a kinda riddle or mystery as to who mighta done it.

They also was gonna make up some music thet would work right in with their singin' school. Since Jill wanted to dance with her swan costume on, they agreed thet would be a good thing fer her to do durin' their singin'.

All the mammas got real busy sewin' an' fixin' up their costumes. The little goslin's had costumes made outta white pillowcases with holes cut outta the bottom corners fer their legs an' some white cotton material over their head with little pieces uv cardboard fer their beaks. Their wings was made with wire an' some more white cloth.

The other costumes fer the other animals was made outta all kinds uv things aroun' the house an' farm, like ol' flour sacks, feed sacks, tow sacks, wire, feathers, an' jest all sorts athings.

But the most beautiful costume uv all was Jill's swan costume, 'cause her mamma knew how disappointed she'd been not gettin' to play Mamma Goose, so she went all out in gettin' Jill's costume made. Hit was made uv a lotta flimsy white cloth with real goose feathers sewed all over hit an' a extra long swan's neck made outta cardboard covered with more flimsy white cloth an' feathers—the kinda cloth folks ordinarily would use fer brides' dresses. I suspicion thet the whole thing got Jill to thinkin' romantic thoughts, but which Jack wouldn't probably be apt to reckanize right then.

Tom's kangaroo outfit was mainly jest a pair o' ol' long john underwear uv his daddy's. His mamma used some onionskin dye to color hit about the color she seen kangaroos in them books. Then she was gonna stuff some newspapers in places where a kangaroo would be filled out more'n jest a ordinary boy. She then sewed up a kangaroo tail an' attached hit in the proper place an' stuffed hit too.

Oh, I fergot to remember thet she also turned the long johns aroun' so the barn door flap would be at the front fer a kangaroo pouch. She even made a little baby kangaroo pillow to put in the pouch. Hit was real cute—almost too cute fer Tom, but he wadn't about to displease his mamma.

Will's big snake python costume was gonna be a little more complicated fer Will to manipulate but in some ways simpler to make, 'cause he, a'course, wouldn't have any arms or legs, jest a long slithery body. His mamma jest got some ol' feed sacks, cut out the ends, an' sewed them together in a long tube-like affair. The bottom end of hit she tapered down into a little point like a snake's tail.

Will wanted to put some rattles on the end uv the tail like a rattlesnake, but Jack objected thet Will had to make up his mind whether he was gonna play a python or a rattlesnake, 'cause he couldn't have hit both ways. Jack then made up thet little sayin', "You cain't have yore cake an' eat it too."

TRICKSTER JACK

Will said, "Cake ain't got nothin' to do with it," but after some arguin' back an' forth an' jest afore fists started flyin', their mamma said thet Jack was right. So after she got the whole thing sewed up with a little stuffin' to fill out the tail end, she painted hit all different colors with dyes she'd made from pokeberry juice, beet tops, goldenrod, walnut hulls, an' red oak tree bark.

Cousin Pete's mamma, what was sister to Jack's mamma, tole Pete she'd need three large tow sacks thet the cows' feed chop had come in. She sewed 'em together in a great big monkey suit with extra large feet an' a rope covered with tow sackin' fer the tail.

Not only was Jack's playactin' role embarrassin' to him, his costume was even more embarrassin', 'cause fer the goose legs, his mamma figgered fer hit to look more right, hit would have to have long pantaloons with frilly lace at the bottom. She thought they'd look appropriate fer the feathered legs uv a goose. The top part was made outta a big ol' white sheet with side pockets sewed in fer the wings. The beak was made outta cardboard like the little goslin's, but a little bigger, a'course.

This gitup uv Jack's costume made the older boys make all kinda fun uv him; but Jack jest kept his countenance, 'cause he already had in mind what their reward was gonna be, an' they wadn't gonna have to wait fer heaven fer thet prize.

After lots uv writin' an' costume makin' an' play practicin', the big night fer the performance was nigh upon them. All durin' the practices, Jack had tried to act as much like a goose as possible by waddlin' aroun' an' aroun' jest like a ol' mamma goose. A'course, this provoked a great deal uv hilarity on the part uv the other chil'ren, but Jack jest didn't seem to pay them no nevermind 'cause he was meditatin' on what Will an' Tom an' Pete had acomin' to them.

Then, oncet in a while, Jack would complain thet the older

boys wadn't doin' a very good job with their parts, makin' out they was those particular critters. He'd say thet Tom's kangaroo needed to hop more often an' a little higher than it seemed he wanted to do. Also he allowed as how Pete, in his gorilla outfit, oughta be pickin' up his feet higher, 'cause the way he was doin' hit wadn't at all funny the way hit oughta be. He said thet he understood thet Will in thet python costume would be sorta uncomfortable, him not havin' no legs nur arms nuther, to negotiate with, don't you know.

"But," Jack sez, "you oughta be slitherin' aroun' a whole lot more than you been adoin'. You jest kinda rollin' aroun', not lookin' like a snake uv any kind, let alone a big long snake like over there in Africa country."

The big night come an' hit seemed like ever'body an' his brother was there. Well, you see, there wadn't a whole lot uv entertainment back in thet day an' time. So folks hadda kinda make up their own fun, hit bein' afore movies an' TV an' even afore radio—at least in them parts.

They started off the performance with some music, an' then the little goslin's did a little dance jest afore Jill in her swan outfit did a real pretty dance what ended up with her flyin' offstage... well, actually tiptoein' offstage to make out like she was flyin'.

The mamma goose (Jack) come waddlin' out tryin' to herd up all the little goslin's, 'cause it'd been rumored thet some fierce critters had been let loose an' was headin' their way. There was a gorilla spied acrost the creek an' he might pick up one uv them little widdy goslin's an' swing with 'em on a big muscadine vine acrost the ocean sea all the way to his own home.

Then there was a quare animal called a *kangaroo* what had a pouch in front uv her belly an' she might could put one uv them goslin's in thet pouch an' head on back to "down under," wherever thet might be. No one seemed to know where "down under" was, but someone had read it in a book.

An' then there was thet long python snake what could swallow whole people alive—even grownups—an' he'd surely be up to swallowin' a dozen or so goslin's.

As Jack was waddlin' aroun' an' aroun' the stage tryin' to shoo them little goslin's, he got the biggest kinda horse laugh at his shenanigans, but he kept right on mimickin' a mamma goose. 'bout thet time all them outlandish varmints jest descended on those barnyard animals an' begun chasin' 'em all over. The chil'ren playin' those parts uv the barnyard critters went scamperin' to escape an you've never seen sech a mess uv leaves an' tree branches an' feathers.

The way they had made up fer the story to go was thet shortly after the foreign beasts was to arrive there would be a kinda chase an' Mamma Goose was to get killed in the melee. They even had a little song about thet:

Who killed the goosey?
Who killed the goosey?
Who killed the goosey,
Bit her in the head?

The goslin's are aweepin',
The goslin's are aweepin',
The goslin's are aweepin',
'cause Mamma Goose is dead.

Actually, thet song hung aroun' a long time, but some schoolteacher named Miss Rhody changed hit to "Go Tell Aunt Rhody."

Then when they was 'bout to find out who killed Mamma

Goose an' afore the doctor was to come in to dose the victim in order fer her to lead them in a little dance with wooden swords, why, hit was then they was supposed to discover thet the python snake was crossed with a spittle snake what could kill abody with a shot uv his spittle.

But now somethin' went wrong, 'cause when the older boys come in playin' their parts they didn't do their parts right. Oh, there was a lot uv real vig'rous movement, but they wadn't sayin' the lines they was supposed to. When Mamma Goose (what was actually Jack) seen them acomin' he, I mean she, did her part an' squawked aroun' quite a bit an' then fell over jest like she's dead, an' there she laid with her head ahangin' to one side an' her legs—all covered with them lacy pantaloons—was stickin' straight up in the air.

What had happened was thet Mamma Goose (Jack a'course) didn't want the boys to get clost enough fer a pretend bite fer he knowed thet his goose was sure enough about to get cooked. A'course he seen right away thet they was doin' the best job imaginable uv mimickin' those storybook animals; better'n they'd ever done at play practice. He knew why they was movin' so believably in their new costumes, an' he realized right off thet they knew what he'd done to them—or at least done to their costumes.

So he figgered if he'd go ahead an' play dead already afore his time (I mean afore his time in the playactin', not his own real lifetime) thet then maybe they'd leave him be... but he was wrong. 'Cause Pete an' Tom, what was playin' the gorilla an' the kangaroo, grabbed aholt uv his legs stickin' straight up there in the air, an' Will, playin' the snake, got aholt uv his tail feathers with his big snake mouth, 'cause you 'member he didn't have no legs n'r arms.

Well, somehower'nother Jack managed to get away from them by scrougin' aroun' ever' which away 'til he broke loose an' started runnin' twarge the door to escape. An' iffen you'd seen them boys chasin' after him down the church aisle you'd been real impressed with their animal movements, but you couldn't know what had so inspired 'em. Jill had a bit uv a notion fer what Jack had tole her earlier to expect a little surprise. The boys, by now, had a pretty good suspicion uv what was influencin' their performance, but only Jack knowed fer sure.

You see, jest afore the playactin' was to begin an afore anyone else had got there, Jack got to those costumes an' doctored them up a bit.

In Cousin Pete's gorilla outfit Jack had put road gravel, an' Pete was sure enough pickin' his feet right up in the air jest like a real McCoy gorilla whenever he'd step down on those gravels.

In the seat uv Tom's kangaroo costume Jack'd put two big handfuls uv cockleburs, an' ever' time Tom went to squat like a kangaroo oughta do, all them cockleburs'd stick his behind an' make him jump like a sure enough jumpin' kangaroo.

Jack was the maddest at Will 'cause he was kinda the leader in railroadin' Jack into havin' to play Mamma Goose. He'd put into Will's outfit a whole load uv poison ivy an' stingin' nettles.

As they went runnin' out the back door of thet church house with Jack's feathers aflyin' an' Pete's feet afloppin' up an' down an' Tom jumpin' thisaway an' thetaway with Will slitherin' along an' ever' inch uv him givin' a awful good imitation uv a big snake, why you couldn't a more set still than all them other folks who was abustin' their sides with laughin' so hard at the goin's-on.

Ever'body later declared thet it was the most comical playactin' they'd ever seen. All but the preacher—he was a little put out with sech hilarity in the church house.

It was after thet thet most folks who knowed Jack, an' what

Jack Plays Mother Goose

he'd done, called him Mother Goose. A'course the older boys called him thet jest to make fun o' him. But most folks called him thet outta sheer admiration. An' from then on all his sayin's an' proverbs an' rhymes an' riddles or any uv the stuff made up about him was all knowed as Mother Goose Tales an' Rhymes.

So you see, Mother Goose wadn't a goose after all an' wadn't a mother nur even a woman. Hit was jest Jack all the time.

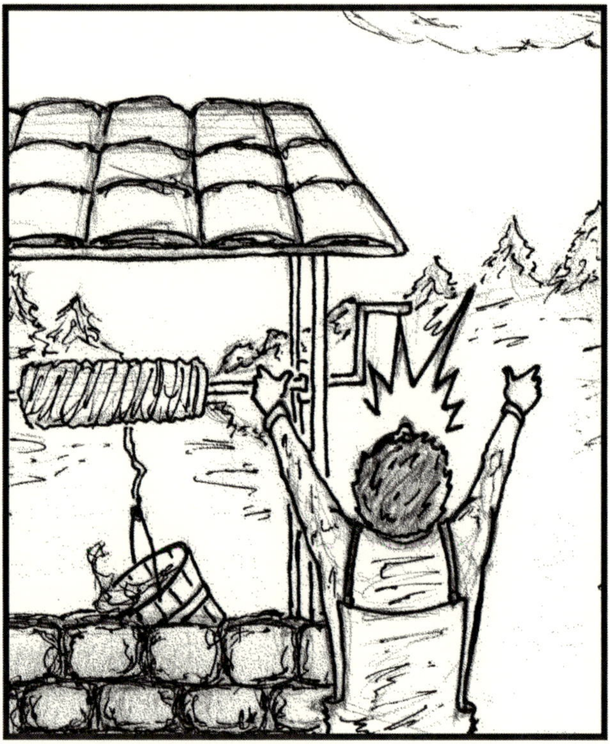

Jack's Childhood Sweetheart

When Jack wadn't much more than jest a teensy fellow, he begun studyin' the girls. All the other boys 'bout his age still thought uv girls as bein' sissy an' not much fun, but Jack was a good deal quicker than the other boys his own age.

There was also a little girl, named Jill, 'bout Jack's age. She too had got past the attitude uv other girls thet boys were all icky. In fact, Jill was so nice thet Jack made up a little rhyme: "Sugar an' spice an ever'thin' nice, thet's what little Jill is made up uv." Her friends didn't like Jack interferin' with their friendship with Jill, an' takin' notice uv Jack's reputation they said, "Snips an' snails an' puppy dog tails, thet's what Jack is made up uv." Hit was later thet some folks changed those sayin's to *what are little girls made out of* an' *what are little boys made out uv*.

Ever' chance the two uv them got they'd get together an' play fun games an' was jest happy bein' with each other. Nuther one uv 'em had siblin's near their own age.

They had all kinda adventures together. Jill could keep up with

Jack whether hit was climbin' trees or wadin' in the river. She'd also grabble in the creek banks fer mud turkles an' run foot races with Jack. He said thet she was better to play with than Tom, his next oldest brother. In fact he made up thet word *tomboy*, which he called her—you see, thet's where thet word come from.

Jack was inventive thet way with words. If a situation or thing didn't have an exact word to describe it, why Jack would haul off an' come up with the appropriate expression.

Jest as Jill would participate in Jack's games, he would likewise play Jill's games like hopscotch an' jump rope, even though she couldn't get him to actually play house nur hold one uv her doll babies.

On one particular day, which didn't seem especially special at the time, they kinda decided about at the same time to go sneak up to Ol' Mr. Hill's new water well an' try out to see if hit tasted any different from the spring water what they was used to.

Even though Jack an' his family, an' most all the other neighbor folks, got their water from a spring, the spring would most o' the times be unhandy to the house. Also, some uv the springs wadn't much more than jest wet weather springs an' would pert near dry up in the hot, dry dog days in August.

Ol' Man Hill lived all alone now thet his chil'ren were all growed up an' moved away. None uv them would live *with*, nur *near* him, no way an' nohow, even on a double-D dare. They hadn't none uv them fergot all the stroppin's he delivered on them when they was still to home. His wife had herself died on him several years afore, 'cause—as ever'one figgered—she jest got tired a-livin' with him an' his triflin' ways.

So now he hadn't got nary a soul to run to the spring fer him an' to fetch a bucket uv water. He had plenty uv money which he'd gouged outta folks one way or 'nother with one deal or 'nother—what was most likely a horse or dog or other varmint deal.

As a matter uv fact, there was one feller who had got the best uv Ol' Man Hill, an' thet was Jack, even though at the time he weren't bigger'n a tadpole when he done it.

Jack's daddy had sometime earlier swapped a coon hound from Ol' Man Hill. His daddy asked Ol' Man Hill, "Now you're positive sure thet this ol' bluetick hound will tree a coon?"

Ol' Man Hill answered right back, "Now I'll tell you fer sure, an' it's the gospel truth, Ol' Tops here"—Tops, thet's what he called him—"why, one night he had solitarily treed a dozen coons even afore midnight. Now if I'm a-lyin' to you, may the lightnin' strike me dead."

Jack had 'membered thet a couple uv years earlier Ol' Man Hill had been struck by lightnin', an' he wondered to hisself if thet was an occasion when Ol' Man Hill had taken a similar oath.

Well Jack tagged along with his brothers, Will an' Tom, when they field-tested Ol' Tops. They found out thet thet dog weren't "tops" in anythin'; all hit'd ever do was eat an' sleep.

Will said, "Iffen I thought I could get by with it I'd swap thet blasted dog right back to Ol' Man Hill an' give him cash to boot, jest to get shet of thet ol' no 'count hound."

Jack didn't say nothin' but started figurin' some way to saddle Ol' Man Hill with thet miserable cur. He thought a minute an' sez to Will, "Why, thet's the very thing, Will, why don't you go on an' do hit?"

Will sez, "We'd never get by doin' somethin' like thet, though there's lots uv folks aroun' here would be tickled pink to see hit done. But even with Ol' Man Hill's squinty eyes, I'm sure he'd reckanize thet it's the same dog."

TRICKSTER JACK

Jack sez, "You want me to go an' do it?"

Will sez, "Why sure, if you think you can bring hit off."

So Jack bought hisself a family-size bottle uv black shoe polish. Then he got a ol' rag an' called Tops an' fed him a fresh hambone, what could occupy his 'tention fer quite a spell. Jack begun spongin' thet black shoe polish all over thet pore ol' dog, 'til he had all the little blue tick specks an' all the white spaces in between completely covered over. Ol' Tops paid no nevermind to Jack's ablutions, 'cause he had all to hisself a hambone what he hadn't needed to steal nur dig up nuther.

Now, Jack got hisself a short rope an' tied hit aroun' thet ol' dog's neck an' then headed over twarge Mr. Hill's place. He figgered if the ol' man saw a new dog a-walkin' past his house, why, he'd jest have to come out an' investigate. O' course Jack made sure hit was a sunny day with no prospects uv rain to rench out his artwork.

An' thet's exactly what he done. Jack made out like he was jest gonna walk right past Ol' Man Hill's, even though he aimed on Mr. Hill a-seein' 'em. He did see 'em an' come—almost runnin'—outta the house an' acrost the porch to get a good look at this unfamiliar pooch.

"Say, Jack," he sez, "I don't recollect a-seein' thet dog in these here parts afore."

"Naw," sez Jack, "Daddy had him *im*-ported from over the mountain somewhere. No one aroun' here has ever seen this here dog—not a-lookin' like this way leastwise." Jack was kinda givin' him a little hint an' also teasin' him at the same time, but the ol' feller didn't catch on atall.

"Say, Jack, thet's a most unusual color fer a dog."

"Yeah, you probably won't find 'nother dog in these parts colored up quite the same as this un."

Jack's Childhood Sweetheart

"Well, now, Jack, what's he good fer?"

"Well now, I'll tell you," sez Jack. "The feller what Daddy got 'im from swore on a stack uv Bibles thet he wuz the best rabbit, 'possum, an' coon dog he ever seen an' he wuz jest as true a dog as the feller wuz his own self. He'd never backtrack nur run a rabbit in the night nur a coon in the daytime. The feller what swapped him to us seemed like the most honest feller you'd ever wanta meet."

"Jack, what'll you take fer 'im?"

"Well, Mr. Hill, I'll tell you what I'll do. I'll take the same money what my daddy paid fer him plus a little extra cash to boot fer groomin' him up so purty."

"Whatcha call 'im, Jack?"

"He answers to the name uv *Spot*."

"That's kinda quare, Jack, an' him with no spots on 'im."

"Yeah," sez Jack, "but we wuz tole he had some blue tick in 'im." Jack had turned the dog's name back'ard from *Tops* to *Spot*, as he thought hit was a most apt name, fer underneath all thet jet black shoe polish there was hundreds uv little speckeldy spots, which all natural blue tick hounds has. Hit was also right—he thought—to turn the dog's name back'ards 'cause uv the underhanded way Ol' Man Hill had dealt with his daddy.

Well, then an' there they closed the deal, but Ol' Man Hill didn't have a chance to try out his new dog afore there was a big gully-washer rain what come an' drenched all thet black shoe polish right offen thet pore ol' blue tick hound's spots.

Ol' Man Hill never got over bein' bested thetaway by a mere schoolboy, an' Jack knew he had hit in fer 'im if he ever showed up agin aroun' his place. He wouldn't a-stood fer hit atall fer Jack to be messin' aroun' his new well box.

TRICKSTER JACK

After goin' over all thet in his mind, Jack sez to the little girl, "We'd better sneak up there real keerful-like, 'cause Ol' Man Hill'll tan my hide if he catches me anywhere aroun' there."

Jill sez, "Well, the well box is on the far side uv the house from the front porch where he's likely to be a-rockin'."

Now a well is a whole lot different from a spring, 'cause in the spring you dip a gourd dipper in the water an' fill up yore bucket. You can also drink right out uv the dipper, if you've a mind to.

A well has a kind uv box built on top uv a wooden platform what is over the top uv the actual well, which would be a round hole maybe thirty to a hundred foot deep. Mr. Hill's well was more than forty foot, all dug by hand, pickaxe, an' dynamite.

Over the top uv the well box is a little wheel, a kinda pulley, what has a rope run over hit with the rope wropped several times aroun' a log type uv affair, at the end uv which is a Z-shaped iron handle. The whole contraption is called a windlass, an' you take aholt uv thet iron handle an' let hit run back'ards to lower the water bucket down to the water. Now the bucket has a metal weight on one side, fastened to one end uv the bale (handle), 'cause if hit didn't have somethin' to tip hit over into the water on one side, why it'd jest set there a-floatin'. You see, hit was a whole lot more complicated than jest dippin' water outta the spring.

But now thet's the way uv progress; things need more complicated tools an' mechanical parts, as well as more experts to run them.

Since the well diggers were experts from over in the next county, Jack had declared, "A expert is a little spurt a long ways from home."

Hit was fer certain thet those young'uns knew nothin' 'bout

Jack's Childhood Sweetheart

how to run this newfangled machine, but, as usual, they'd try it anyhow, an' as Jack'd say, "Come heck ur high water." You see, Jack wadn't 'lowed to use swear words like "hell" an' "dam" 'ceptin if he's talkin' 'bout where the devil lived or backin' up water in a branch or creek.

So when they opened the top uv thet well box to let the bucket down, they paid no 'tention to the iron handle on the end uv the windlass. Hit went fairly flyin' an whirrin' aroun' an' hit Jack clear in the top uv the head. Blood jest spurted out all over place, coverin' his face like a Halloween mask. He was kind addled by thet, but he started runnin' to home with his little girlfriend right in behind him.

When he got home his mamma made a poultice uv vinegar an' brown paper to go over the cracked an' bleedin' part uv his skull. In them days brown paper was used a lot fer the makin' uv a poultice on which you might put vinegar, pepper, or even mustard or whatever, 'pendin' on the type uv ailment hit was.

Now if you had a chest cold, they'd put brown paper with mustard an' a hot wet towel over yore chest to draw the cold out. Sometimes fer sore eyes—like uv a mornin' when yore eyes were matted together with sleep drippin's—your mamma'd scrape a Arish (Irish) 'tater an' put the scrapin's in a clean white cotton cloth an' put thet over the bad eye, which'd clear right up. Fer boils or carbuncles or bee stings or other skin ailments, you'd use wetted down bakin' soda or new mixed red mud. But the best treatment fer thet kinda thing was ambeer (fresh-chewed chewin' tobacco).

In Jack's case with a busted head, his mamma put on brown paper soaked in apple cider vinegar, what was intended to take out the swellin', stop the bleedin' an' achin', an' prevent any infection. What self-respectin' bacteria would want to be soused with a dose uv vinegar thetaway?

After hit was all over, Will an' Tom started teasin' Jack 'bout the whole ordeal, particularly 'bout him likin' thet little girl, Jill, so much. Well, both Tom an' Will kept after Jack with their joshin' him, 'til Will, who wadn't ordinarily a hand to write anythin', made up a little rhyme 'bout hit. Hit went somethin' like this:

> Jack an' Jill went to Ol' Man Hill's
> To draw a bucket of water.
> Jack was conked on the crown
> An' he fell down
> Jill knew thet they hadn't oughter.

Some fellers in a big school over yonders a way got aholt uv Will's poem an' changed hit a good deal. They writ the first part uv the poem to read:

> Jack an' Jill
> Went up the hill
> To fetch a pail ….

I reckon they jest fergot Ol' Man Hill's name, but in the first place, a body would commonly go down the hill to fetch water—not up—'cause ever'body knows water runs downhill—even underground—to springs an' branches an' creeks.

But those rewriters couldn't let well enough alone 'bout Will's well poem. Jack jest figgered they was some more little spurts uv experts, 'cause they was from a long ways away. Hit jest goes to show you thet there's nothin' sacred anymores—someone's allus messin' aroun' with what somebody else said or wrote.

Jack's Childhood Sweetheart

Jack wadn't at all pleased 'bout Will makin' up thet little poem 'bout him an' Jill, so he made up in his own mind to get even with his brothers somehow, but he wadn't sure yet jest how he'd go 'bout it. He figgered hit'd come to him later.

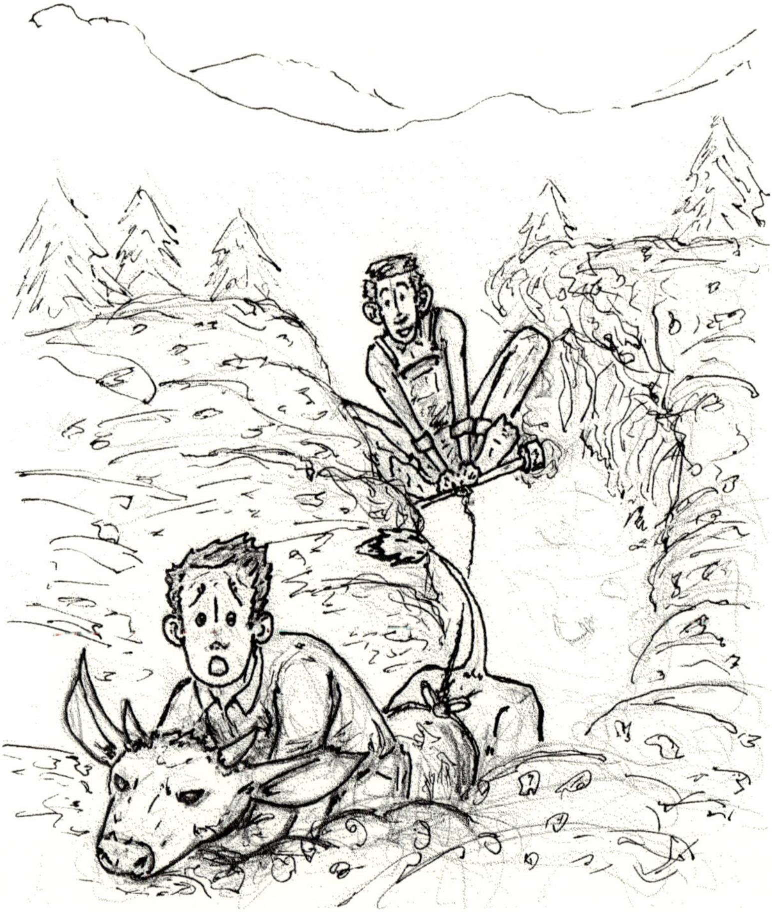

Jack's New Wagon

Bout the time Jack turned eleven he decided he was gonna make hisself a little wooden wagon to pull Jill aroun' in an' maybe ride down a slope like you would on a sled when snow an' ice would be on the ground.

When he started workin' on it, he asked both Will an' Tom to help him, but they jest teased him thet much more when he jest wanted thet little wagon to pull Jill aroun' in. Thet was when Jack made up thet story about the little red hen wantin' someone to help with plantin' a grain uv wheat. So Jack said then jest like the little red hen, "Well I'll jest do hit my own self." an' thet's what he done.

Jack was now even more determined to build the blamed thing, so he located some red oak boards an' nails an' rope (for pullin' or steerin'). Then he got the one-man crosscut saw to saw off four white oak tree trunk ends about two inches thick fer wheels.

He made hisself a list of things he needed like a kind of recipe:

TRICKSTER JACK

(2) 22" x 2" x 2"
(2) 35" x 6" x 1"
(1) 35" x 4" x 1"
(4) 8" (diameter) x 2" (tree trunk ends fer wheels)
(1) 6' rope
(10) washers
(4) cotter pins
(3) 10" x 1" x 2" (for bracin')
Nails
Axle grease or lard
(1) 4" stove bolt & nut (for steerin' pin)

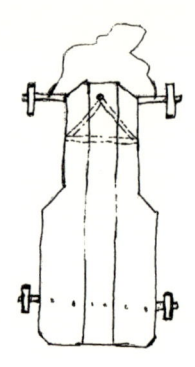

After he got the whole thing finished, he realized thet there wadn't a clear place anywhere to ride the thing down a hill. Now there was a kind uv slope what woulda been ideal if hit hadn't abeen so growed up with bresh an' brambles an' briers, but hit would take a whole lot uv cuttin' an' diggin' to get hit all cleared out enough to ride down hit in his new wagon.

So hit come to him right then an' there how Will was gonna assist, if not in buildin' the wagon, at least with clearin' out a kind uv roadway fer the wagon to run, even if Will was gonna do hit unintentionally—sorta involuntarily, so to speak.

So Jack asked Will if he had yet rode thet yearlin' bull calf, what they called Thunder—'cause as a calf he had already showed promise as a real bull roarer. Will looked at him kinda suspicioned-like an' said thet he hadn't any notion thet yearlin' bull could be rode afore he was actually broke to be rode. He was also takin' into account how the bull had allus been pretty wild when yet a runt calf.

Will was reminded by Jack how he his own self had broke to ride thet young stallion what Uncle George had sold to their daddy

Jack's New Wagon

last spring an' what ever'body was skeered uv. They named him White Lightnin', not jest because uv his color an' speed, but also 'cause thet was what people called thet dangerous hooch which people got into trouble with the revenooers about.

You see, what Jack'd done—an' him no more'n ten years old at the time—unbeknownst to anybody, was to get into the barn loft above thet stallion's stall an' let down a horse collar over thet horse's midriff where a saddle would ordinarily go. Now when thet horse collar clamped in aroun' White Lightnin's ribs somewhat like a man's legs aridin' him, why thet horse got to snortin' an' buckin' an' rearin' somethin' terrible an' kickin' at the barn staves, nearly kickin' some uv 'em out.

Jack conducted this little ritual at least once a day, well nigh onto a month, 'til thet stallion quieted down real pussycat-like whenever Jack was close by, 'cause Jack allus rewarded his improved behavior with a lump uv sugar whenever he would get the horse collar offen his back.

Then one day when Uncle George was there, Jack got on White Lightnin' bareback an' rid him right out the pasture gate with Uncle George an' ever'body else yellin' after him to get off thet wild horse afore he got hisself plumb kilt. Now Jack was remindin' Will to remember all thet.

"Now," sez Jack, "that's what I done with thet yearlin' bull, an' he rides as gentle as a summer breeze." Jack was lyin' a'course, but he wadn't above tellin' a fib once in a while when hit suited his purposes. On the other hand, Will hadn't seen Jack doin' all thet with Thunder, but then, come to think uv it, he hadn't seen Jack breakin' White Lightnin' nuther. What he could remember was last spring when Thunder was no more'n two months old an' how feisty he'd been then.

Ever'body'd still laugh when they'd recollect how Cousin Susie tried to befriend thet little feller by leadin' him with a short rope down to the branch fer water, an' how thet little bull calf got to jumpin' real frisky-like, scarin' Susie, who kept tryin' to say sweet things to him to calm him down. You see, Susie figgered she could solve all the problems in the world, iffen she could jest find the right sweet thing to say in any kind uv contentiousness.

If she couldn't find the right sweet thing to say in a situation she'd resort to swearin'—by haulin' off an' jest yellin', "Dadburn hit!" O' course she'd say nothin' worse than "Dadburn hit anyway" or "Confound the darn thing," but she'd say hit with sech vehemence, you'd swear she's cussin' like a sailor, an' when she hollered one uv her nasties, nobody'd want to be standin' close by. She was a caution!

Now about the time she started tryin' to cajole thet bull calf by sayin' sweet things to him, he started "feelin' his oats" by kickin' up his hoofs an' runnin' twarge her. Susie yelled, "Confound thet durn thing, anyhow!" an' dropped the rope an' taken off runnin'. Little Thunder wadn't bein' obstreperous, he jest thought she's aplayin', so he took off right behind her, an' when she looked over her shoulder, there he was no more'n two jumps behind. So she run faster an' faster an' so did he.

When Susie come to a big poplar tree at the edge uv the field, she wadn't lookin' back no more an' jest grabbed aholt uv the trunk of thet tree an' shinnied up the tree like a squirrel on the first day uv huntin' season. She set there on the bottom limb of thet poplar tree 'bout twelve foot off the ground 'til the boys had corralled up thet little bull calf. Afterwards, Jack tried to get Susie to climb thet tree agin, but she couldn't get more'n a couple afeet off the ground—she was missin' the inspiration uv Thunder.

Jack's New Wagon

Will 'membered thet about Cousin Susie an' the little bull calf, but he also realized thet Thunder had grown up to yearlin' size now, an' he hadn't seemed to get any gentler—in fact, he'd chased several growed men outta the bullpen. Then agin, on the other hand, he figgered it'd really be somethin' to brag about if he could ride thet yearlin' bull like Jack had rode White Lightnin' the year afore.

Will said thet yeah he'd do hit if he had a little time to tell Tom an' run acrost the creek to norate (narrate) to the Ayers boys thet he was gonna break Thunder to ride. Jack said, "Yeah! Sure!" 'cause he wadn't ready his own self right then to go get the bull.

While Will went to round up Tom an' go fetch the Ayers boys an' some other fellers, Jack got out his little wagon an' put hit right at the head of thet slope, what was all covered with bresh an' sech. When Will came back with his cheerin' section uv a audience, Jack had tied a roped yoke aroun' Thunder's neck an' led him up to the top uv the slope what he wanted cleared out.

Though the yearlin' minded Jack pretty much when he was aleadin' him, Jack knew he wouldn't tolerate anythin' on his back. 'Cause he had, in fact, tried thet horse collar trick on Thunder, but hit didn't work atall, and he didn't do hit the second time. So hit wadn't a outright lie what Jack had tole Will 'bout doin' the same thing with Thunder thet he'd done with White Lightnin'. But hit surely hadn't worked with the yearlin'.

Will was workin' up his audience about how he was gonna 'complish this feat an' thinkin' at the same time how he was assured thet Jack had already done the job. Jack was busy hitchin' the rope uv his wagon to the rope yoke aroun' Thunder's neck.

Now when Will jumped on thet yearlin' bull's back, Jack jumped onto his new wagon, an' they all three—Jack 'n' Will 'n' Thunder—went tearin' down thet hillside. an' when I say tearin', I mean tearin', 'cause with Will bouncin' on Thunder's back an' Jack in thet little wagon behind, they was tearin' everythin' offen thet slope: the briers, the brambles, an' even some young saplin's. Thet bull, as wild as he was, wadn't gonna go straight to anywheres, but kept acrisscrossin' the slope, mowin' hit all down. Jack had figgered he would somehow head down the hill twarge the branch where he was used to goin' fer water, an' thet's exactly what Thunder done.

O' course on his way down he'd kicked up his heels, throwed his head back an' forth, an' bucked his back, turnin' first to the left, then to the right, atryin' to dislodge Will. But pore Will didn't dare let go fer fear Thunder would stomp on him, an' if thet didn't happen then Jack in his infernal new wagon would tromp on him, runnin' right over him.

Will was a-screamin' to beat the band. All the boys in the peanut gallery was laughin' an' yellin'. Jack was havin' the time uv his life, ahollerin', "Get up there, Bucky Boy! Gee in there now. Haw now!" A'course thet bull didn't know gee from haw. "Keep agoin', Thunder Boy."

By the time Jack 'n' Will 'n' Thunder 'n' the new wagon was to the bottom uv the hill, all thet rarin' an' runnin' an' jumpin' an' kickin' had cleared the whole slope uv all the underbresh. Jack sure had hisself a clear way all the way down thet hillside to ride his new wagon.

Pore Will had taken sech an unexpected whippin' in the whole

Jack's New Wagon

episode thet Jack sang a little song inspired by the evenin' song uv whippoorwills.

> Whip pore Will!
> Whip pore Will!
> Why do you whip pore Willy so?
> That is what I'd like to know.
> Whip pore Will!

It was then thet Jack publicly thanked Will fer the new highway fer his brand new wagon an' announced so thet ever'body would know, "Where there's a *Will* there's a way."

This new way what was involuntarily contributed by Will was gonna be jest the very thing fer Jack to give Jill a joyride in his spankin' brand new wagon, an' when they'd get to the branch at the bottom uv Will's Hill they could jest douse their feet in the branch water fer wadin' or go crawdaddin'.

As a kinda afterthought uv the whole experience, Jack invented a new play-pretty, what some folks call a folk toy, an' he named hit Thunder Roll. The other boys called hit a bullroarer.

You make hit by cuttin' a real thin board like a lathin', about a foot long an' two inches wide. With yore jackknife you round off all four corners, then punch a hole in one end. You find a real stout cord, 'bout five foot long, an' tie hit into the hole you've jest punched.

When you take ahold uv the end of thet cord an' swing hit aroun' yore head, the board starts flutterin' an' sounds jest like a bull a-roarin'. Hit become real popular with the other chil'ren, particularly the boys.

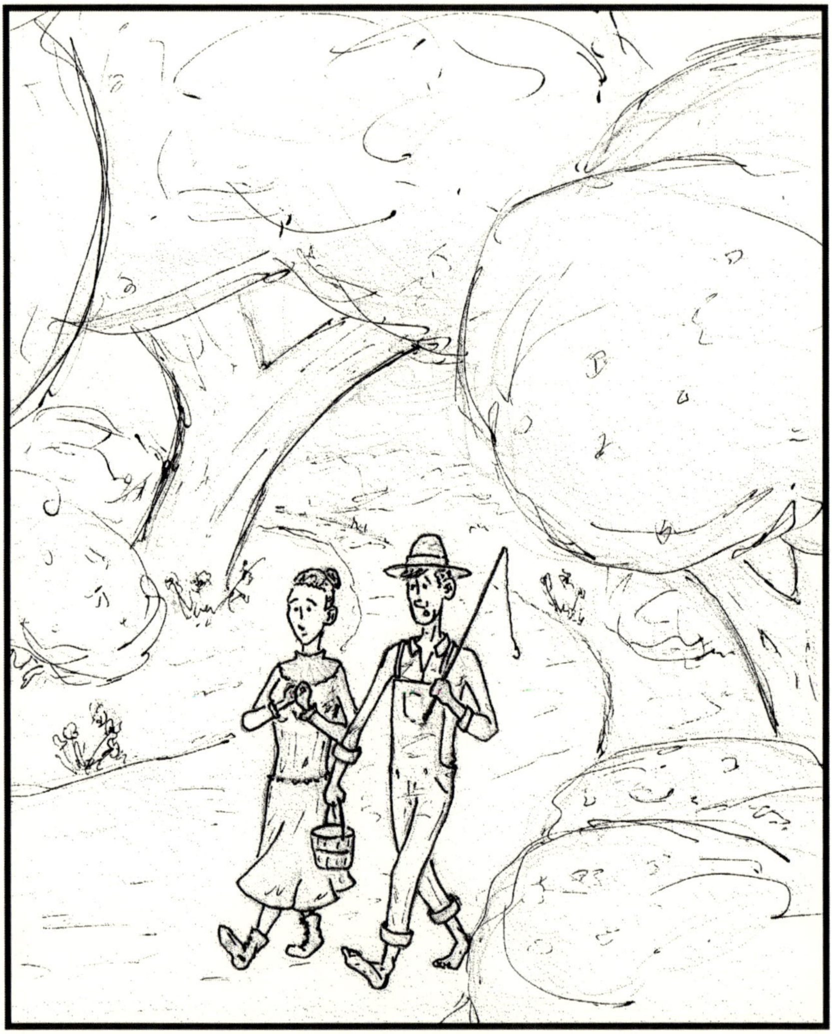

Jack's End of a Romance

When Jack an' his sweetheart begun to get a little older—too old fer hopscotch an' jump rope an' sech—they still liked to kinda hang out together an' do special things like go on picnics an' other adventures.

Oncet they took off fer to go fishin', but they didn't want to let on to nobody else where they was goin'. So they didn't get the proper hooks an' poles an' sech where folks would see from all thet stuff thet they was headin' fer a little romantical trip down by the river. Actually they didn't make up their minds about goin' fishin' until they was almost halfway there to the fishin' hole.

Then when they agreed thet's where they's aheadin', Jack said he'd cut a fishin' pole with his jackknife. Boys an' men back in them days allus carried a knife in their overhaul pockets fer any sech emergency as cuttin' fishin' poles. In fact, if a boy's daddy found out thet his boy had neglected to have his knife with him, why he was most likely in fer a whuppin'.

While Jack was to cut a pole, Jill was to turn over some rocks down there on the river bank to find some fishin' worms. A'course, they'd also need some string, an' Jack allus had a ball uv tobacco twine, what he'd saved from strippin' the tobacco leaves fer market after it's been flue-cured in the barn. A ball uv string might come in handy fer lots uv things like a baseball or even fishin' line.

The way you'd make a baseball was to find yourself a little rock—jest a tad bigger'n the end joint uv yore thumb—an' then you'd use thet string you saved from the cured tobacco. None uv the pieces uv twine was very long, but after you'd wound one piece aroun' the rock a few times, why then, you'd tie the end of thet string to the end uv another string an' then jest keep on a tyin' an' on an' on until you'd have a satisfactory-sized baseball.

There was allus plenty uv twine, 'cause it'd never be used the second time fer tyin' the green tobacco, fer if you did, hit might not hold durin' the curin' the second time aroun' an' then drop on the hot flue pipe an' maybe catch the whole barn on fire.

Now in Jack's day an' neighborhood they'd never heard the word "recyclin'," but thet's what they done most uv the time. The sole uv a wore-out shoe might become the business end uv a fly swatter. Used empty feed sacks was awful handy fer shirts an' skirts as well as dresses an' aperns. Ol' newspapers could be cut in strips, hung over a stick, an' used to fan the flies offen the table, an' was often used to paper the inside uv the house fer both insulation an' nighttime readin'—even if hit was ol' news.

So Jack allus carried, in addition to his jackknife, several other useful little articles, what might come in handy fer all sorts uv jobs an situations. He allus had thet ball uv string too, but you had to be kinda careful with thet ball, 'cause you gotta 'member thet the core of hit was a rock, an' you sure wouldn't wanna get hit by thet thing, particularly when some of thet string had unwound from the rock.

Jack's End of a Romance

Jill had been a-scroungin' aroun' there on the river bank, turnin' over rocks, an' had found at least a dozen real long juicy fishin' worms, what was destined to make prime fishin' bait. Now they—the two uv them—figgered they had ever'thin' they needed fer fishin' 'cept a fishhook. She had one uv them newfangled foldin' pins, what they call a "safety pin," holdin' the straps uv her sunbonnet together.

Jack taken the pin an' bent hit to make out like hit was a fishhook, an' then tied some string through thet little hole at the head uv the pin. He then rolled 'bout ten foot of thet string offen the twine ball an' tied thet other end to the pole thet he'd whacked off a yellow poplar tree branch hangin' there over the water.

When hit come to baitin' the hook with them fish worms what she'd already picked up, why Jill was jest a little squeamish 'bout stickin' thet crooked pin through their innards. Jack done the manly duty an' impaled the little critter his own self.

They found a place to set an' fish, right offen a gnarly root uv a ol' sycamore tree what was bendin' out there over a deep water hole in the river.

Jack took the first turn at throwin' in the fishin' line; he'd already learned thet in thet day an' time hit was the man's obligation to go afore the woman. A'course, in most parts uv the world today it's most polite to let the lady go first in things, but in Jack's place hit was deemed wise to have the man go first fer walkin' down a path or takin' a drink uv spring water, fer safety's sake, don't you know, particularly under circumstances like the path or spring bein' unknown.

Well, as luck would have it, by time Jack had throwed thet fishhook in the water thet worm was clear gone. Then thet little girl, right then an' there, said, "Let me try thet thing." So she let Jack put another worm on thet safety pin, an' she dropped thet line in the water right next to a big ol' chestnut log what had lodged itself in there from the last rain flood. She thought she felt a nibble, an' she jerked hit outta the water, but the hook didn't have a fish an' agin didn't have a worm.

They kept takin' turns doin' this until they'd lost all the worms. They couldn't tell whether the fish had stolen them or they had jest slipped offen the pins their own selves, 'cause there was no proper hook like what was on the store-boughten ones to keep them hooked into place.

After thet they jest took to playin' aroun' with sticks an' leaves, makin' little hats an' bonnets. Then they found some flat rocks, what could be used fer skippin' acrost the water. They would count how many times a particular rock would skip afore hit baptized itself into the river. Jack counted one uv his rocks as many as seven times. Jill counted hers up to eight, but Jack was jubous (dubious) about thet an' was reluctant to 'knowledge hit.

The fact is thet Jack got real worked up over her beatin' him in thet rock skippin', an' he was noticeably unsettled. She declared thet she hadn't cheated at all, an' besides hit didn't differ thet much whether she had more skips or he did. He allowed hit sure did make a difference, him bein' a boy an' all. An' ever' boy has his pride at doin' things like runnin' an' climbin' an' throwin' an' even skippin' stones acrost the water.

She was 'bout to come back at him with some kinda argument when he stood up real sudden-like an' lost his balance right over into thet fishin' hole. While he was asputterin' an' asplashin' aroun' gettin' outta there, she offered him a hand, but he wadn't gonna take another insult to his manhood. She got so tickled over the whole thing thet she almost fell in her own self.

By the time he pulled hisself out, she reckoned right out loud thet "a boy's pride goes afore a fall into the river." Even though hit wadn't his sayin', an' he didn't even wanta hear it, he was the inspiration fer hit more or less: "Pride goeth afore a fall."

That was the first fallin' out they ever had, even though there were times when each uv 'em would get on each other's nerves. Well, to tell the truth there was a little incident what had happened not so long afore thet, but hit wadn't exactly a fallin' out even if she did slap him.

Well, you see, what had happened was they was down by the river settin' on their favorite rock there, watchin' an listenin' to the river, when Jack jest up an' sez, "I betcha a nickel I can kiss you without touchin' you." Now he wadn't bein' romanitical atall; he was jest bein' a smart aleck, athinkin' he could pull one over on her. Now with her hit was different. She had begun to think lovey things 'bout her an' Jack—an' not them same ol' ever'day things like fishin' an' sech.

So she studied real hard what he said he would bet 'bout kissin' her without touchin' her; she especially studied 'bout the kissin' part, 'cause Jack hadn't let on atall to her thet he's the least bit innerested in thet kinda thing. An' he wadn't innerested really; he jest wanted to have some fun at her expense by playin' a little joke on her.

She sez, "Now I don't see how a body can kiss a person an' not touch them. Hit jest don't stand to reason."

Jack sez, he sez, "Is hit a bet or not?"

She wanted in the worst way to see how he could do thet without touchin' her, so she sez, she sez, "Sure enough it's a bet."

So Jack grabbed aholt uv her an' planted a great big juicy kiss right on her lips. She couldn't say she didn't enjoy it, but she did say, "But you touched me."

Jack reached in his overhaul pocket an' fetched out a nickel an' handed hit to her an' said,

"Yep! Hit sure was worth hit."

Then she hauled off an' slapped him right acrost the face, not 'cause she hadn't enjoyed it, but 'cause hit was jest a big joke fer Jack with no romantic feelin's in hit atall fer him. Actually, she thought hit was kinda cute uv him to do thet, but she woulda hoped fer hit to have a little more meanin' than jest a boyish joke.

After the fishin' hole dunkin' an' their little fallin' out, what didn't amount to much an' didn't last long, Jill got to yearnin' more an' more fer Jack to pay more 'tention in a boy-girl way. But he jest kept on atreatin' her like one uv the fellers, even though she was a kinda special feller.

They was both 'bout fifteen years old by then, an' Jill got to studyin' more an' more on marryin' 'cause her older sisters an' most uv the other girls she knew had started courtin' an' marryin' 'bout thet age. But if she was waitin' fer her best friend, Jack, to start thinkin' 'bout romance or sech permanent things as marriage, she was gonna have to wait a long time.

But one day right outta the blue, when they was standin' down by the river, Jack made up a little song. Now, she was a'course used to Jack makin' up little sayin's an' riddles an' rhymes an' sech. Ever'body knew he was a great hand at thet sorta thing, but they was usually jest some clever notion uv his or some outlandish tale.

This little song was different; at least hit begun different with a kinda sweetheart feelin'. Hit went somethin' like this:

Hello, little girl, hello, hello!
Hello, little girl, hello!"

She was pleased as punch, so she answers right back in the same tune:

Hello, little boy, hello, hello!
Hello, little boy, hello!

Then Jack sung:

Let's set, little girl, let's set, let's set!
Let's set, little girl, let's set!

She answered:

OK, little boy, OK, OK!
OK. little boy, OK!

They set down right on thet big rock near the fishin' hole an' Jack kept right on asingin' as he leaned over twarge Jill:

A kiss, little girl, a kiss, a kiss!
A kiss, little girl, a kiss!

She was waitin' fer him; not thet she wouldn't have been happy with a kiss, but this seemed like the right time an' timin' to test the waters fer Jack's notions 'bout future ceremonies like weddin's:

Let's sing, little boy, let's sing, let's sing!
For a kiss little boy, a ring!

Now Jack was taken aback by her songwritin', an' hit took him a couple seconds to recover:

Goodbye, little girl, goodbye, goodbye

You see she had jest skeered the bejeebers outta him, an' she knew it, but jest to go along with his fun, she joined in the last line uv his song, an' even harmonized with him:

Goodbye, little (boy/girl) goodbye!

It was also a kinda goodbye from both uv them to their childhood.

When she noted how jumpy he was when she sung 'bout a weddin' ring, even if hit was jest in fun, she thought maybe she'd better start lookin' aroun' fer other more likely prospects. Thet was when she started talkin' with Billy Caudle.

After she married up with Billy, Jack was kinda saddened but philosophical nevertheless 'bout the whole thing. He missed her somethin' terrible, but consoled hisself by sayin', "Well, it's probably better to have loved than not to've ever loved."

It's been said thet some writer over yonder in London town wrote out thet sayin' uv Jack's like, "'Tis better to have loved an' lost than never to have loved at all." Then a feller would memorize thet an' say hit on a play-actin' stage. They still orate thet to this day.

That same writer feller wrote out on his own behalf:

If this be error and upon me proved,
I never writ nor no man ever loved.

You see, thet furren feller writ down words jest like Jack done.

A Penny Saved

Now one day when Jack was almost nearly growed up he was headed home from playin' ball with the other boys over to Abe Handy's cow pasture. He was feelin' pretty smart, 'cause he had hit his first home run ever. He was goin' over in his mind all the details uv his great moment:

All the others, even Will an' Tom, his two older brothers, was yellin' him on into home plate, which was jest a slab uv a plankin' board.

However, jest as he was roundin' the third base, which was jest a dried cow pie, he'd stepped in a fresh one, an' hit looked like the Ayers boys was gonna get the ball back outta the creek in time to tag him out. But he jumped up startin' to do a barnyard dance to wipe the nasties off his bare feet an all 'twixt his toes, an' you know what hit feels like to step barefoot in squishy mud puddles.

The boys had started in a-yellin' aroun' 'im an' pushin' him on twarge home plate.

"Hurry hit up, Jack!"

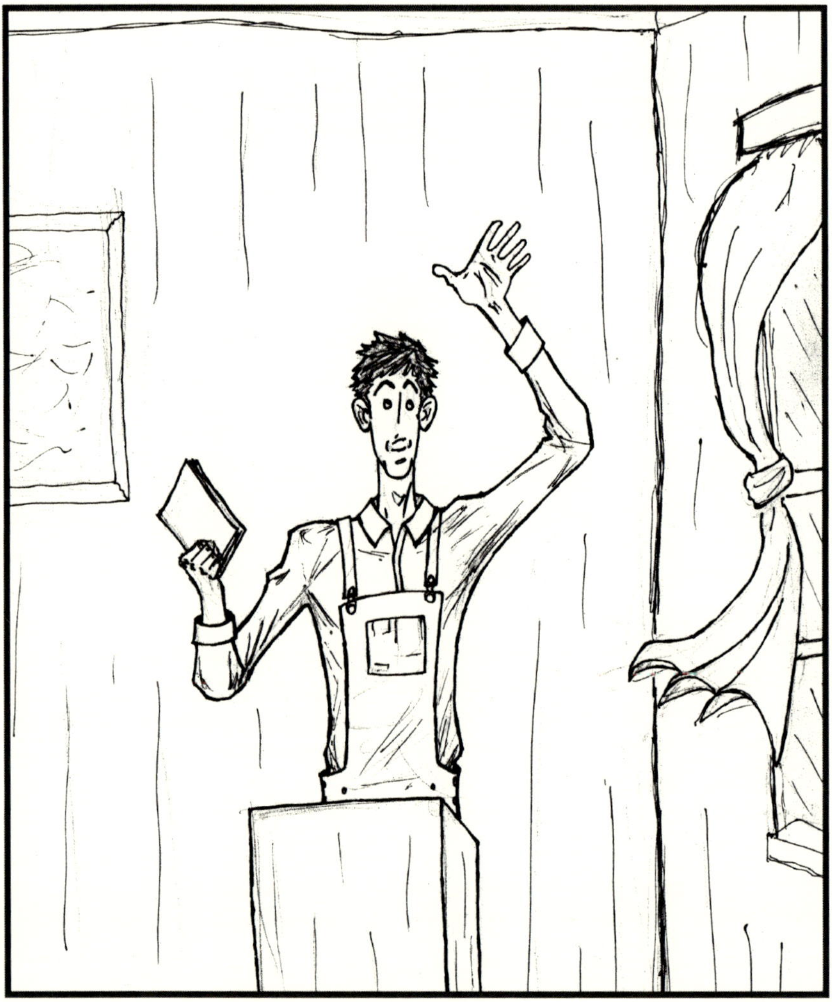

A Penny Saved

"Git the lead outta yore britches!"

"We ain't got 'til Christmas!"

"This'll be the winnin' run iffen they don't ketch you out!"

Then they started in teasin' him: "I knowed you was partial to Christmas pies an' plum puddin's, but I never knowed you had sech a hankerin' fer cow pie."

"Hey, Jack, I got a whole tow sack fulla sheep pellets; you might like to go with yore cow pie."

"Yeah, Jack, we got loads uv chicken droppin's in the henhouse."

Jack was a-thinkin' hit was a bless-ed thing thet he hadn't awore his new mail-order brogan shoes, what he'd a thought about wearin' to show off in front uv them other fellers. O' course, if he'd a-done thet an' stepped in thet cow pie with new brogans on, he'd a got aswitchin' fer sure from his mamma when he'd agot home.

Well, by now ever'body was worried 'bout him finishin' the run in time; Toby Ayers had throwed the ball outta the creek to Robert Ayers, who dropped it, 'cause the twine ball was plumb soaked with creek water what splashed all over Robert's face. But he picked hit up real quick-like an' throwed hit to Aubrey Ayers at the pitcher's mound.

Jack had finished cleanin' hisself up an' was headin agin twarge home plate where he run clear over Cleve Ayers, the catcher, jest as he was reachin' to catch the ball. But pore Cleve with Jack runnin' over him like thet an' thet string ball bein' still wet an' slippery with the creek water, why he jest couldn't hold onto hit.

So Jack got hisself a bonyfidy homerun—not countin' errors, an' creeks an' cow pies.

After Jack's homerun ever'body gathered up real clost to him, tellin' him how skeered they'd been thet he might not finish the run in time. He jest made out like he'd taken all the time in the world, 'cause he was so all-fired confident in hisself thet he'd make hit.

Will said, "Why, little brothah, I was jest sure thet you'd never..." Jack cut him off jest as sharp as a frog gig: "Don't never say never, 'cause never never goes to ever! Later is allus better than never, an' in this case it's a home run."

So after thet all the boys started yellin' aroun', "Later is better than never; later is better than never!" An' then they'd laugh real big. A'course, if there's other people standin' aroun' who hadn't been at the ball doin's, why they'd jest think the boys'd been nippin' a little or maybe jest a smidgen touched.

But now, ever since thet time, people would, from time to time—when hit seemed a thing might be gettin' a little late—why they'd jest dig up thet little wisdom uv Jack's: "Better late than never!"

Right after the conclusion uv the ball game, the Ayers' boys went mopin' off with their tails atween their legs, 'cause this was the first time in three summers thet any other team had been able to beat 'em. Jack's team headed into town, where there was a frolic rumored fer later on thet night.

Not Jack. He headed in home, 'cause hit was his turn to do the milkin' thet evenin'. He was walkin' by the old Willow Creek Primitive Baptist Church jest as he seen a terrible lookin' thunderstorm headin' twarge him, so he decided he'd better duck in the church house an' wait out the storm.

A'course in those days, nobody ever locked the church house—it didn't even have a lock to be locked—'cause church folks figgered there might be times an' circumstances when someone might need to come into the church house fer a meetin' or thinkin' or prayin' or maybe even comin' in outta the storm uv some sort. There wadn't any worry 'bout somebody stealin' anythin' out uv it, 'cause the benches an' other furnishin's was too big fer abody to fool with an' who'd think somebody might be liable to steal a pulpit? There wadn't any songbooks, 'cause only the preachers would have songbooks, what they'd use to line each song an' let the congregation sing the line after the preacher had intoned it. So there's no songbooks to steal.

While Jack was standin' there in the doorway, waitin' fer the lightnin' an' thunder to let up, an' kinda thinkin' 'bout how trustin' all the folks thereabouts was, he noticed somebody else headin' fer the church house an' jest splittin' down the road to get outta the rain his own self.

Now wouldn't hit be the curiousest thing, but hit was the very feller what had begun to cause lots afolks to mistrust, 'cause he'd been known to cause a lot uv commotion aroun' lately. Jack reckanized right away thet hit was the highway robber what had been hangin' aroun' there uv late.

Although Jack was feelin' mighty smart 'bout thet ball game, he wadn't quite ready to tangle with thet rogue—not right then, anyway.

The lightnin' was gettin' closter, an' Jack saw an' heard it hit a big red oak on the hill acrost the road from the church house. So he had to make a quick choice—encounter the outlaw or dive into the storm.

As usual, Jack didn't take the options handed to him—he hastened up to set in the preacher's big chair behind the pulpit, where he figgered he'd be completely hidden from sight uv the robber—it bein' so dark an' all from the thunderstorm.

When the rogue jumped into the doorway he tried shakin' the water offen his clothes; in fact, he even took off his shirt an' started wringin' hit out—you know like twistin' a twist uv chawin' 'baccer leaves. Hit was rainin' thet hard to jest soak a body to the bone.

Then all uv a suddent thet feller spied Jack asettin' real easy-like up there in the preacher's chair, an' hit skeered him 'cause he couldn't tell who Jack was—you know, him asettin' up there so calm jest like he knowed ever'thin' what might be agoin' on roun' there. So the rogue suspicioned thet Jack could be either the devil or an angel uv God settin' up there, an' either one uv them would have been bad news fer him right then an' there in his present condition uv roguery.

The ol' robber didn't let on atall thet he was the least bit nervous. He was also a sorta con man, don't you know. So he sez real mean-like, "Hey feller, what kinda yahoo are you? I reckon you must be the devil settin' up there so big an' proud. I bet you even got cloven hooves." His vig'rous slappin' on his leg an' his out-loud laugh at his joke kinda covered over any feelin's uv unsureness he mighta been havin'.

Jack set on there real still, jest atryin' to scheme out what'n all he was gonna do to get outta this predicament.

While Jack was jest settin' there like a stone statue, thet rogue sez kinda under his breath, "Well, I guess a feller oughta give even the devil his due."

He didn't think Jack heard him, but hit started Jack in thinkin' what he'd meant by doo, after his own earlier experience at the ball game. Hit was only years later thet Jack continued thet sayin', "You gotta give the devil his due," which he'd figgered out meant to give even the devil what's rightfully acomin' to him.

A Penny Saved

Now Jack was feelin' a little queasy settin' up there in the preacher's chair where he'd never been afore, an' hit did give him a kinda quare feelin'. But Jack spoke right up jest as big as you please, jest like he wadn't skeered atall of thet ol' robber man. "Why," he sez, "I'm Saint Peter! The Good Lord sent me down to check on folks in these here parts 'cause He's abeen hearin' a lot uv bad reports on certain people aroun' here, an' He sent me down to investigate the goin's on an' what kind o' devilment might need to be set straight."

Now this made the ol' robber a little oneasy, realizin' you know thet he'd been astealin' an' a roguin' aroun' in this neighborhood fer quite a spell, but he still wadn't about to show thet he was gettin' a little worrisome.

So he spoke right back to Jack, "Well, if you're St. Peter an' not the devil, why're you asettin' up there jest like a preacher man?"

"Well," Jack answered right back, "I had some information thet there was a highway robber messin' 'round in here, an' hit might be appointed right about this time fer him to come down this public road: so I tole the Good Lord thet a thunderstorm might be the very thing to set our purposes right."

Now thet rogue wadn't gonna let on atall thet he was gettin' jest a tetch jumpy, so he kept on bluffin' when he said, "How do I know you're St. Pete an' not some mischief maker comin' up with all this hyar foolishness?"

Jack shot right back at him, "I guess you'll jest hafta take my word fer hit."

But the robber didn't waste no time in sayin', "I don't never take nothin' off nobody, nohow." Now I'm atellin' you, he was a' ornery cuss.

Jack, jest as nimble, sez, "I guess the God Amighty might wanta hear 'bout thet."

So the robber sez, "Well, I'm agonna call yore hand on this un" (which means to put yore cards on the table to see who the winner uv the card game might be). The ol' rogue goes on asayin', "I heard thet St. Peter was a pretty pow'ful preacher. Is thet right?"

Jack figgered he might as well agree an' doin' so wouldn't lose him any cards, not in this hand anyway. So he sez, "Oh yes, I held some mighty pow'ful tent meetin's in my day."

"Well then," said the robber man, "Why don't you jest haul off an' start preachin' right now, 'cause you're standin' in the right place." (By this time Jack had got outta the preacher's big chair an' was standin' behind the pulpit) "An' if you're who you say you are, why I'm in the proper notion fer some good preachin'."

Jack was put on the spot sure enough now, so he thought he might buy hisself some time by askin' the rogue if he had a special scripture passage what St. Peter might expound on.

The ol' rogue said, "Hit don't differ none atall with me. Hit's been quite a spell since I heard any preachin' an' to tell the truth I was never learnt to read scripture my own self."

Jack was in a real bind now, 'cause he couldn't recall any scripture either as he said to hisself, *Hit's been a month uv Sundays since I been to meetin'*. But hit then come to him thet he might get by jest recitin' any old sing-songy pattern uv words what might pass fer the unusual words an' rhymy quality uv some uv the scripture what he could dimly remember.

The only thing he could think back on was thet little teasin' song what'd been made up against him so many years ago. So Jack sez to hisself, *I've a mind to use thet ol' Jack Horner rhyme an' hope he don't notice the difference from real scripture, 'cause unless I disremember it, hit was kinda sing-songy too.*

Now afore he started his make-believe preachin' he stepped

up onto a overturned Coca-Cola crate what was right behind the pulpit fer short preachers to stand on. He didn't really need the soda pop crate, but when he all uv a sudden got taller an' started in usin' his voice like the real preachers, why, thet rogue really set up an' took notice. An' when Jack ordered him down to the front bench where St. Peter could keep a eye on him, why, he didn't waste no time atall in obeyin', then quieted down jest like little baby chicks when a chicken hawk is circlin' overhead.

Then Jack looked down onto the top uv the pulpit like he was readin' directly from the Good Book itself an' commenced as he lifted his eyes heavenward an' raised his voice to the church steeple:

> Little Jack Horner sat in a corner
> Eatin' his Christmas pie.
> He stuck in his thumb
> An' pulled out a plum,
> An' said "What a good boy am I!"

By time he'd finished quotin' he was flailin' his arms an' boomin' his voice like he'd observed from the real preachers. The ol' robber couldn't exactly recall where or whether he'd ever heard thet scripture, but then he hadn't heard much uv any scripture afore, an' this assuredly didn't sound like yore ever'day ordinary talkin'.

Now, when Jack diverted his eyes from heaven an' looked down on his congregation uv one lonely pore soul an' taken notice thet he was payin' real strict 'tention to the scripture readin', why thet jest inspired Jack on into the spirit uv the whole thing. He fergot all about gettin' skeered an' jest let her rip, particularly when he heard the fellow uncock his pistol an' lay hit down with a thump on the wooden bench.

He kept right on with his preachin'. "Now thet little feller, Jack, he was asettin' in the corner. He wadn't a high-falutin' type uv feller asettin' out there in the middle uv the floor. Naw, he was asettin' in the corner...jest a meek little tad uv a boy...wadn't actin' biggedy atall. Why hit reminds me uv my own dear chilehood, an' maybe some uv you folks in the congregation" (as if there was a whole passel uv folks there) "...maybe hit remembers you back to yore own innocent chilehood."

Jack heard a small sob from his congregation uv one, an' this seemed to lift him onto the wings uv heavenly angels like a song he had already made up, "Wind Beneath My Wings," an' jest added fuel to his fire, so to speak—but I ferget myself an' realize thet the fire is in the other direction.

As Jack kept agoin' on an' agoin' on, ever oncet in awhile he'd hear a Amen, as if there's a real Amen corner, an' more than one sob to denote a full house on the mourner's bench.

Now when Jack really warmed up to thet pretend Bible preachin' an' reminded the congregation thet thet little boy had said, "What a good boy am I!" the sinner man on the front pew groaned a little as Jack continued:

"Now, dear friends, those uv you under the inspiration uv my voice this mornin'" (Fergettin' hit was afternoon), "I ask each an' ever' one uv you to ask yourself in direst honesty if you can rightly say, 'What a good boy am I!'?"

Rememberin' real quick-like thet he was supposed to be St. Peter, why Jack said, "Now when I was awalkin' here on the yearth an' afore I was called to handle the keys to the Kingdom, I was jest like all you sinner folks an' worldly people out there. You been athinkin' meanness, you been atalkin' meanness, an' you been adoin' meanness." The ol' robber was acryin' an' amenin' at the same time,

A Penny Saved

but Jack went right on, "An the Good Lord is tired uv hearin' 'bout hit."

At about thet time the sinner man was on his feet an' aheadin' twarge Jack, which skeered the bejeebers outta him, but he held his ground.

An' jest when the rogue got in front uv the pulpit he fell on his knees, asobbin' an asayin', "I believe! I believe! St. Peter have mercy!"

Now when thet robber come runnin' up twarge him, why, Jack temporarily fergot thet he was supposed to be St. Peter. He was kinda stunned fer a minute there—until the robber quit lookin' at the floor an' looked up to St. Peter, so Jack come to hisself real quick then an' sez to the robber/sinner, "Mister, hit sure looks like you jest got yourself saved."

"Oh, St. Peter, yes. Yore preachin' has tetched my heart an' made me see my wicked ways."

"Well," sez Jack, "What's yore name?" The robber looks real suspicious at Jack, but Jack reckanized right off his mistake an' said, "Not thet we don't already know yore name, 'cause it's already writ in thet big book, what you a'course already know 'bout. It's jest thet we gotta test yore veracity." (Jack had heard the real preachers usin' thet word.) "You gotta be honest with me now"—pretendin' his own self thet he was honestly St. Peter (even though a young one).

"Oh, St. Pete," the ol' robber sez, "I know what you're a-talkin' about. My name is Jeems...Jeems Penny."

He slowly looked down twarge his feet jest when a hailstone, then another an' then another, hit the churchbell—hit was still stormin', don't you know—an' thet robber, Jeems Penny, looked up with his eyes jest a glowerin'. Jack was afeered thet the bulgin' eyes was a indication thet his own time was jest about up. He even thought to hisself, *Now who is thet bell tollin' for; maybe fer me.* Some feller, years later, writ hit down but changin' the words to "The bell tolls fer thee."

Jack even listened fer awhile to see if the tolls numbered his age. Whenever a body in the neighborhood would die, someone'd ring the church bell as many times as the age uv the person. Thet's what "The bells toll fer thee" means. He didn't keep countin', 'cause other things started happenin'.

Mr. Penny—when he heard the hailstones ringin' the church bell an' nobody pullin' the bell rope—why, he thought his own self thet his time was up an' the Lord was callin' St. Peter to hurry on back with his new convert in tow.

Hit was right then thet lightnin' hit the church steeple an' rung the bell fer sure. Hit was later reported thet the bell could be heard all the way over into the next holler. The thunder shook the church house walls an' rattled the roof shingles. A ball uv fire rolled down the bell rope up the center aisle twarge the pulpit—jest missin' Jack an' the rogue—an' out the open winder. This skeered the liver outta both o' those liars.

Now some folks would call these events jest happenstance, but the Primitive Baptists woulda said hit was destined to be this way an' serves both those rogues jest right fer their devilments.

Well now, Jeems Penny was so frightened he whirled aroun' an' headed back to the pew at the back uv the church fer his hat, an' by the time he'd turned his back on Jack, why Jack made fer the winder behind the pulpit, jumpin' out right into the rain an' hailstones an' all, although the storm had let up a little bit. The fireball, a'course, was already gone an' the thunder had quit echoin' up an' down the holler.

A Penny Saved

Jack was convinced thet maybe Penny was headin' back to the pew to get his gun, or also maybe the Good Lord was unhappy with Jack's outlandish prank fer sure this time. Either one uv those circumstances woulda been uncomfortable, so thet's why he literally jumped outta thet situation.

Now when the sinner man picked up his hat what was layin' there on the pew right next to his gun an' then looked aroun', he didn't see Jack or St. Peter—jest a empty space with a kind o' glow behind the pulpit. He was surely now convinced thet Jack was, in fact, St. Peter, an' had been called back real quick to take care uv some heavenly business.

But the new convert was indeed grateful thet he, his own self, was spared fer a little more time here on the yearth afore receivin' his heavenly reward. So he put on his hat an' headed outta there an' never bothered nobody aroun' there anymore.

When folks would talk about him, some said he come from Richmond an' others said Roanoke, but most folks was convinced he was a Yankee. They was all convinced thet he musta been, indeed, a changed man, 'cause come next meetin' day, his gun was found on the back pew still loaded but uncocked.

The real preacher, Brother Hiatt, decided he oughta take it fer his own personal protection, don't you know, an' he figgered further thet he'd keep hit outta the hands uv another rogue.

Now when Jack norated the whole thing to the boys, he declared thet he was "in a real pickle" an' couldn't figger how to end the whole episode until the hailstones an' then the lightnin' hit the church bell, an' he said, "Jeems Penny may have been saved by grace, but I was surely saved by the bell." Now thet's where thet ol'-time sayin' come from, "Saved by the bell."

Though we don't know 'bout his soul, Jack's hide had surely

been saved thet day from a good tannin' or a good shootin' if thet feller had found out 'bout who he really was an' him pretendin' to be St. Peter an' a genu-wine preacher at thet.

Jack made up a little sayin' about the whole experience. 'Cause the rogue's name was Penny, Jack said, "A Penny saved is a lesson learned." He had certainly learned his lesson not to pretend to be a saint nor a preacher ever agin.

Whenever someone tole the town banker about thet sayin', why, he got hit a little mixed up—him bein' a little deaf an' his own onnatcheral mind allus on money—he repeated hit as, "A penny saved is a penny earned," an' put hit over the door uv the bank. Nobody remembers anymore what Jack actually said about savin' Jeems Penny.

Will, Jack's oldest brother, was so taken with the whole story thet he named his favorite black layin' hen—what was also a good settin' hen—Henny Penny. I believe hit was one uv his young'uns what made up thet little rhyme:

Henny Penny, my black hen;
She lays eggs for gentlemen;
Sometimes nine, sometimes ten;
Henny Penny, my black hen.

After the banker put up his sign, other stores started mimickin' him by advertisin' their businesses. The tailor put up a sign: "A stitch in time saves nine." Nobody knew exactly what hit meant, but hit sounded nice. The terbaccer store put up a sign what read, "Don't chew yore tobacco twice, come to us fer a new chewy twist." The beauty parlor's sign said, "Beauty is in the eye uv the beholder." thet prompted the eye doctor to put up a sign with a big eye in the middle, right under gold letterin': "Seein' is believin'." thet gold letterin' prompted the jeweler to put up, "All thet glitters is not gold, but our gold is guaranteed to glitter."

The horse trader put up, "You don't look a gift horse in the mouth, but you can read our horses' teeth any time atall." What thet meant was, you could tell a horse's age by lookin' at his teeth—it was a sight to see men pullin' up the lips uv the horses jest afore a big stock auction. But if abody was to give you a horse you wouldn't count its teeth to check the quality or age uv yore gift. Thet'd be downright rude.

The town barber put up a sign: "A close shave is good fer a smile." Hit later got changed to "A miss is good as a mile."

Now hit cain't honestly be said thet Jack come up directly with all those slogans thet went into those store signs, but indirectly, unbeknownst even to his own self, he had somethin' to do with ever' last one uv them by inspirin' them with his encounter with thet robber man.

You might even say thet Jack invented outdoor advertisin', an' if the whole truth be known, he more than likely had a hand in the whole beginnin' uv the business uv capitalism.

I don't know if he'd lay claim to thet or not.

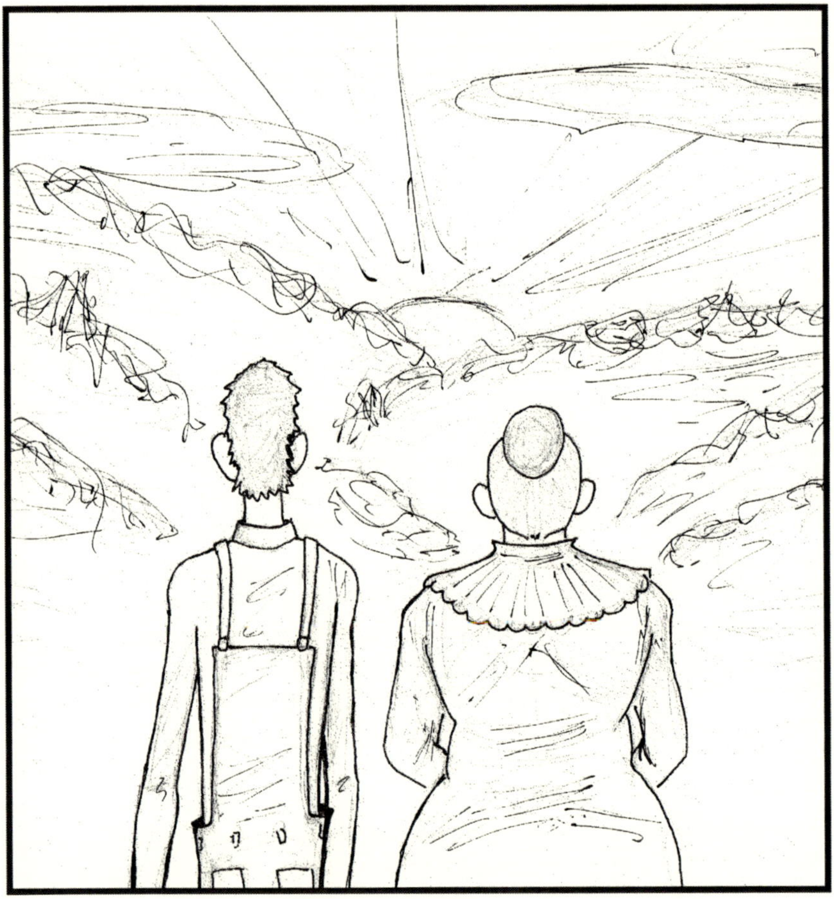

Jack's Diet

After Jack an' Lorene got married an' he started in foremanin' down to the sawmill, things went along pretty good fer them, but you know how things start gettin' after a couple gets married; they both get settled down in their own particular—and sometimes peculiar—ways. Fer them... hit was jest thet they kinda developed different tastes.

Afore Jack had begun his new job an' his new marriage, he was real handy to do all kinda things—from carpenterin' to tobacco farmin', from diggin' ditches to breakin' horses an' mules. He'd even been a lumberjack fer a while... thet's how he'd named it—"lumber-jack." He'd also been a jack-tar (sailor) fer a short spell. How thet got the "tar" part of hit was thet hit was his job to daub tar in any holes what might develop in the ship's hull.

He was pretty good at a lot uv trades but hadn't really 'prenticed to any one master tradesman. Hit was his brother, Tom, what started thet sayin' about him, "Jack-of-all-trades, but master uv none." Jack didn't seem to take exception to thet. I don't think hit bothered him none. He seemed to take hit as meanin' a lot uv folks in general an' not jest hisself in particular.

Right after the weddin', Jack took to cookin' an' was 'specially good at fixin' rabbit stew. As a matter uv fact, he was so good at it, an' people enjoyed hit so much at potluck dinners, thet folks got to callin' hit Jack's rabbit stew. After thet the rabbit itself become known as "jackrabbit." You see, thet's where the word jackrabbit come from.

In addition to rabbit stew, he was noted fer cookin' up big batches uv other stews an' soups in a big iron pot. He become so famous fer his pots full uv good vittles thet hit become known as a "jackpot," an' even today when there's a whole heap uv somethin' good what might be won in a card game or gamblin' or prize hit's called a jackpot.

Hit was when Jack was workin' at the lumber camp, afore him an' Lorene got married, thet he had his first chance to do some cookin'. How hit happened was thet the reg'lar cook had a bad case uv tremblin's after a long weekend in town. So the boss asked Jack if he might could cook the ham an' eggs an' biscuits fer breakfast. Jack allowed as how he'd learned all thet from his mamma, but in truth, he really didn't know how to mix up the bread dough.

When he put all the fixin's in a humongous mixin' bowl, he poured in way too much milk—more like a thick soup than any kinda bread dough. He got real sloppy with hit an' spilled some right on the top uv the hot cookstove. A'course hit startin' right in a sizzlin' an' makin' little bubbles. He quick took a big meat cleaver to pick hit up to keep hit from stickin' to the stovetop. When he done thet, hit flapped upside down right over onto the other side. He noticed thet the top side now was nice an' brown, so he picked

Jack's Diet

hit up agin with the meat cleaver an' dumped hit into a plate settin' on the end uv the stove.

Albert, who was on the cleanup crew, sez, "Jack, what in tarnation is thet flattened out thang?"

Jack—not wantin' to own up to a mistake he mighta made—said, "Oh hit's jest a flap..." (an a'course hit had flapped out on the stovetop) "Hit's jest a flap I invented here while scramblin' up some eggs."

"Well, Jack, what do you put on the blamed thang to make hit fittin' to eat?"

"You might jest put on some butter an' pour some uv thet molasses on it, 'fore you stuff pieces of it in yore mouth."

That's what Albert done an' right off yelled, "Would you whip up another one uv them flaps, Jack?"

Other fellers started gatherin' aroun', wantin' to take a bite uv thet flap, Jack.

Now thet's how Jack cooked up the first flapjack, which has become popular over most uv the civilized world, an named fer him, "flapjack," as a kinda commemoration, don't you know.

Jack had allus liked hog-butcherin' time. In addition to neighbors an' kinfolks comin' over an' helpin' out like at thrashin's, there'd be fresh meat an' big dinners with canned an' root-cellar provisions from harvestin'.

As Will was the oldest an' most pow'ful uv the three boys, he'd be the one assigned to kill the hog what was destined to carry the family through the winter months. Because uv Will's strength, Jack invented a word fer thet: "willpower." Now hit seems ever'body is innersted in willpower—their own willpower, I mean.

After the hog'd been killed an' bled, hit'd have to be gutted, an' thet allus seemed to be a problem. Jack figgered a way to heist (hoist) the carcass by puttin' a kinda lever under hit. Folks then called thet a "jack." An' you know, to this day, people still call thet a jack fer automobiles an' sech. After hit was heisted up thetaway, then hit'd be hung on a block an' tickle (tackle) fer takin' out the innards fer fried up chitlin's. After cleanin' 'em out real good, they'd be real tasty, iffen they're fixed right. You hadda make sure you didn't cut into them wrong, or you'd ruin all the meat. Jack figgered out how to hang hit right, an' hit reminded some uv the older folks uv bygone days when highway robbers or murderers would be hung. Although Jack didn't invent the hangin' uv rogues, they did begin to call a hangman a "jack ketch."

Actually before the eviscleratin', the pig carcass'd hafta be dehaired. Jack was real handy with scrapin' off the hair an' seasonin' the different cuts uv meat. There was a special way what would be used to cut the hair off. You had a big metal vat full uv water over a hot fire, an' when thet water got to aboilin' real vig'rous-like, several men would take aholt of thet pig carcass with meat hooks attached to the leg tendons an' dip him real sudden into the scaldin' water—not enough to start cookin' the meat but enough to soften the bristle-hairs. After you'd pulled it out, then you'd take a old zinc metal lid offen a Mason cannin' jar an' scrape acrost the hairs, which the scaldin' water had softened up, don't you know.

It was somewhat like shavin' the whiskers offen yore face after you'd softened them with hot water an' some good lathery lye soap.

Jack's Diet

Now Jack an' his neighbors never saved the hog hairs, but they was some folks what would save the pig bristles, which they said was used to make a pretty fair paintbrush.

It was claimed in them days thet when you butchered hogs you saved ever'thin' but the squeal. Some boys would even save the pig tail, wrap hit in Christmas paper, an' put hit anonymously under the Christmas tree fer a special girl.

Now I cain't think why they thought any girl would do anythin' but squeal with horror when the pig tail was unwrapped at the school Christmas party. Even though Jack would do a lot uv devilish things, he'd never stoop so low as thet.

On hog-killin' day itself, his mamma'd cook up the liver fer liver puddin' with special seasonin's fer to be sliced later fer sandwiches fer school lunches.

Jack loved grindin' up a kinda balance uv lean an' fat in the sausage grinder with some special seasonin's. Then they'd cut up the fatback in little pieces—savin' some fer cookin' with pinto beans—then cut the skin offen them so's they could be cooked in a big iron pot on a outdoor fire to render the lard to be used fer fryin' later on.

The pigskins would be stuck in a hot oven on a cookie tin an' saved fer huntin' trips or other occasions when cookin' was inconvenient, but eatin' was necessary an' somethin' real tasty would be mighty welcome. The little nubbins uv fatback—after all the lard had been cooked out—would be put aside to be put into cornbread batter fer cracklin' cornbread.

The tenderloin was the strip uv lean meat down each side uv the backbone, an' a mess of hit would be cooked up on hog-killin' day itself, but was mostly canned fer the cold days uv winter.

Jack loved workin' over the hams an' shoulders with a good deal uv salt, pepper, brown sugar, an' other curin' seasons, an' wrappin'

TRICKSTER JACK

them in a cotton cloth to be hung up in the smokehouse, which had a fire pit underneath fer smokin' hit an' givin' hit a nice smoky flavor.

At times they didn't smoke hit but jest let hit hang until hit was properly cured fer a coupla months at least, an' maybe more if you really wanted the ol'-timey cured country ham flavor.

When Jack helped neighbors he was usually rewarded with the hog's head fer souse meat, the feet fer pickled pig's feet, an' the innards which he'd cook up fer chitlin's, what some folks later would call tripe. He seemed to be satisfied with thet, as he was particularly fond uv pickled pig's feet.

Howsomever, after he got his new job when he'd be offered a hog-killin' job fer the payment uv the pig's feet an' sech, he'd declare, "I'm livin' high on the hog nowadays," which he was, 'cause he could afford the higher-up portions like the hams an' shoulders, what with his new job an' his new wife. Whenever you hear someone sayin' "livin' high on the hog," whether they're sayin' hit 'bout their ownselves or somebody else, they mean they're able to afford the more expensive cuts uv meat sech as the hams an' shoulders an' tenderloins.

But thet little sayin kinda caught on 'cause uv Jack, an' even Jack swore he wadn't 'bout to be "gettin' above his raisin'"—a sayin' thet a lot uv daddies picked up from Jack when their own offspring was about to leave home to seek their own fortune.

Now, Lorene was a whole different story altogether. Afore she married Jack she was real spoiled by her folks—her daddy bein' the doctor an' all—an' she never had to do anythin' aroun' the house or on the farm. But after she married Jack she taken to cookin', 'cause she knew ever'body had to've had a occupation no matter if you was rich or poor.

Jack's Diet

That satisfied Jack jest fine, 'cause he fer certain did like eatin' but never seemed to gain a pound. He stayed skinny as a rail even after several years uv Lorene's cookin'. His Uncle Buck said thet he ate so much thet hit made him skinny jest carryin' hit aroun'. A'course he never ate any uv the fat what Lorene was jest silly about. The eatin' arrangement seemed to work out tolably well, 'cept Lorene got to gainin' weight with all thet fat in her diet.

Now this worked out real good when they fried the country ham, fer which they used a big iron skillet. After fryin' hit Lorene would cut off the fat fer her own self an' save the lean part fer Jack, which suited him jest fine.

Then after the meat was took outta the skillet, she would make a little redeye gravy by pourin' a bit uv coffee into the leftover grease in the pan, then pourin' thet into a little pitcher to be poured later over the white-sop gravy, what was made by siftin' a little flour over the remainin' ham drippin's in the pan.

She'd stir thet flour aroun' in the ham fat until hit browned, then she'd pour about a cup uv fresh milk into thet browned gravy until hit boiled a little. Thet'd be some mighty tasty country ham white-sop gravy what'd be poured over some hot biscuits an' their portions uv the meat—Jack's bein' the lean an' Lorene's bein' the fat.

Then over thet they'd pour some of thet set-aside redeye gravy. The reason hit's called redeye gravy is thet when you pour thet coffee into the ham drippin's hit doesn't mix real well an' hit looks kinda like a redeye lookin' up at you when you pour hit over the white-sop gravy. Another reason, I've heard tell, why it's called redeye gravy is when you eat hit uv a mornin' after you get up ayawnin' an' with puffy red eyes, particularly after a night afore uv whatever; why then those ham fixin's with the redeye gravy does somethin' miraculous fer the sleepiness an' redeyes an' all.

TRICKSTER JACK

Now I've gotta quit talkin' about thet country ham an' redeye gravy, 'cause I'm beginnin' to smell them fixin's what I've not had in a long while my own self.

When you cook with a iron skillet this way, particularly fer country ham an' redeye gravy an' white-sop gravy, there's no leavin's in the pan, so's to clean hit you jest wrench hit in some cold water while it's still hot, an' you won't have to really warsh hit atall—it's already cleaned itself. I'm sure ever'body already knows you'd never try to clean a good iron skillet with any kinda soap. If you did, someone'd jest have to cure hit all over agin with grease in a good hot oven.

Jack's brother Tom made up another rhyme about Jack an' Lorene an' their particular arrangement uv vittles:

No fat for Jack
That was a fact.
No lean
For fat Lorene.
'twixt the both of them
They cooked the skillet clean.

Later writers added Sprat to Jack's name jest to make a rhyme, then fergot Lorene's name altogether, jest namin' her "wife," an' changed the name "skillet to "platter."

Jack Sprat
Could eat no fat.
His wife could eat no lean
So betwixt the two of them
They licked the platter clean.

Jack's Diet

You see, they even made out thet Jack an' Lorene "licked" the platter, throwin' off on them like thet jest 'cause they was mountain folks.

But now thet's what happens sometimes with those ol' sayin's; somebody allus has a better idee uv how they oughta go.

Ol' Jack

Nobody seems to 'member 'bout Jack as he begun to get older. I s'pose it's 'cause when rapscallion boys grow up they most uv the time turn into gnarly grumpy ol' curmudgeons. But abody oughta note thet the agin' uv impish boys into grown-up men is jest like the curin' uv good country ham or the maturin' uv vintage blackberry wine. As Jack would say, "Hit jest gets better with time."

Jack had allus taken to frog giggin' an' was real partial to good fried bullfrog legs. Oncet when he was younger, he put the bullfrogs in the icebox without dressin' 'em—what means cleanin' an' skinnin' 'em—an' the next mornin' when his mamma opened up the big icebox lid, some uv them bullfrogs had revived an' jumped right out, acroakin' right at his mamma.

She fainted plum dead away. A'course she come to after they sprinkled a little water on her. Jack had neglected to teach them frogs to "look afore you leap." Or to tell his mamma, "Look afore *they* leap."

TRICKSTER JACK

When Jack was older an' more responsible he made sure to dress his frogs right away after giggin' 'em. When him an' some other fellers was afixin' to fry some frog legs in a big iron skillet over a campfire, he salted the legs, what looked like a little man's legs with their bulgin' thighs an' calves. But he'd fergot thet when you salt frog legs they get to quiverin' an' ashakin'.

He musta salted one pair o' legs too much, 'cause they jumped right outta the pan. Jack declared, "Outta the fryin' pan an' into the fire!" Ever since then when a body tries to get outta one hot spot but ends up in a hotter spot, you might hear somebody say, "Outta the pan an' into the fire."

The older Ol' Jack got, the fewer pranks he pulled but the more stories he tole uv his pranks an' tall tales, particularly to his own grandchil'ren. At the end uv ever' story he'd rar back , stop whittlin', an' proclaim, "An' I swan (swear) thet thet's the actual fact or I'm a monkey's uncle."

Now I don't know when he started thet expression, 'cept when he was younger, when him an' his brothers went to the circus an' seen the monkeys jumpin' aroun' all over the place. I believe hit was Will what said, "I do declar', Jack, if them monkeys don't put me in mind uv you."

Tom said, "Naw, don't lay off on Jack thetaway. He's too cantankerous fer a measly monkey; he's gotta be at least a monkey's uncle."

So after thet, ever' time Jack wanted to guarantee the veracity uv a thing he'd said, he'd clinch the argument with "or I'm a monkey's uncle."

In the days when Jack was still a young man, folks'd raise hogs out in the woods an' not bother atall with fences. Well, the ol' razorback pigs woulda rooted underneath any fence anyway. When

Ol' Jack

folks years later did start puttin' their pigs in fences they'd clamp a little brass ring at the top edge uv their nose, so thet when they'd start rootin', the sharp points on the ring would dig into their nose flesh, painin' them enough to quit.

The hogs in them days wadn't fleshy like nowadays. They had real pointy noses an' was even called razorbacks 'cause they had sech sharp ridge backs.

A'course some uv the lazy farmers with fences wouldn't feed their hogs enough, an' they'd have to root out to get some vittles on their own. Thet's when Jack advised some ol' skinny razorbacks uv Mr. Hill's, "Sometimes you gotta root, hog, or die."

That sayin' would sometimes be brought up when abody might be counselin' some pore soul: "Root, hog, or die," which means to get on with it, whatever it may be.

What Jack'd do to reckanize his hogs when he turned 'em loose thetaway in the woods on the mountainside, he'd cut a certain kinda notch in his pigs' ears. Then when it'd come hog-killin' time, he'd jest go out there an' identify his pig brute.

The reason he didn't hafta feed the pigs was thet there was enough mast, like acorns, beechnuts, hick'ry nuts, chinkypins (a small nut what grows on bushes), an' sech, to feed 'em year-roun'.

One year Ol' Jack went huntin' fer his ol' Bangus Boar (what he called him) after the "frost was on the punkin" an' all the 'simmons had been tickled by Jack Frost. (Now I could stop right here an' tell you how Jack Frost got thet name, but I don't want to bother with a hist'ry lesson right now.)

When Ol' Jack would later tell his grandchil'ren about thet adventure he'd norate (narrate) hit this way:

"You see, I'd heered thet Ol' Bangus had been a rootin' up the whole hillside up there on Saplin' Ridge, an' I'd caught a glimpse uv him a coupla times when I's up in thet direction asquirrel huntin'. An' the best I could make out from what I'd seed uv him was thet he was a right smart-size hog. Well, I wancha to know I tracked some mighty big hoof prints in the snow, which I opined thet hit mighta been a horse, but the hoofprints was split, so I figgered then hit musta been a cow.

"Then I seen 'im, an' at first I thought hit was a black bear. But I taken a look at thet right ear an' knowed right then an' there thet hit was Ol' Bangus, so I slipped up behind him an' grabbed him by the tail, wroppin' thet curly tail right aroun' my wrist.

"But, you know, thet hog took off from there, tearin' through the underbrush, but I wadn't 'bout to let go. He run on an' run on, an' I was gettin' 'bout tired out when I seen him headin' straight twarge a big shag bark hick'ry tree.

"I figgered he'd closed his eyes an' wadn't payin' no 'tention where he's runnin' an' was gonna run right into thet blamed tree. So I reckoned agin in my own mind thet thet hick'ry was gonna stop him fer sure.

"You know, when he hit thet tree, his sharp pointy nose split it in two jest like a rivin' axe, an' he run right through thet hick'ry with me still hangin' on. But, don'tcha know, by time I was nearly through the tree them two split parts sprung back together an' grabbed my coattail, an' I hung there fer three days, 'til a search party come out an' foun' me.

"I sure was cold an' hungry.

"Yes, yes, an' thet's the actual fact, or I'm a monkey's uncle."

One uv his grandkids said, "Papa, why didn't you jest shuck yoreself outta yer coat?"

Ol' Jack didn't say nothin'. He jest blinked a coupla times an' started in whittlin' agin real fast, tryin' to take no notice thet some uv his younger kin might be as sharp as he was.

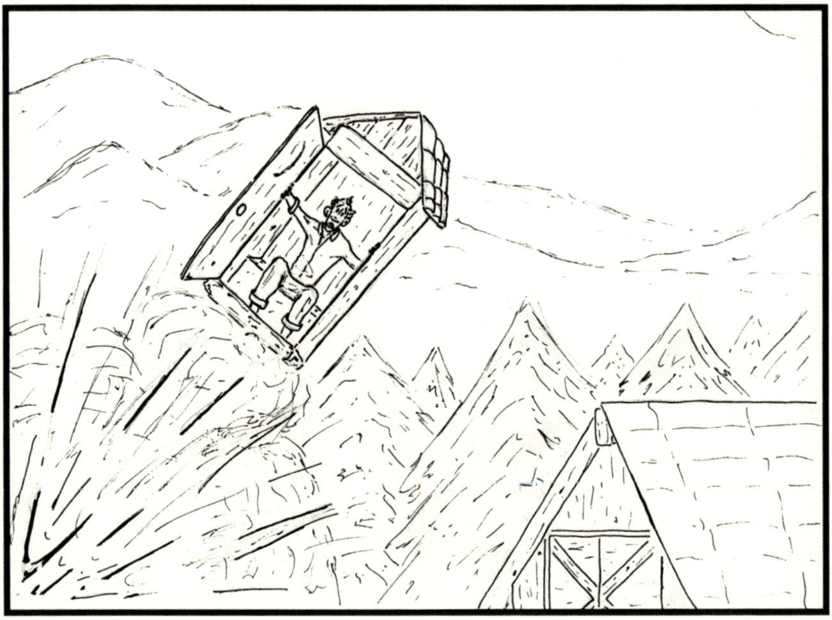

Ol' Jack's Indoor-Outhouse

Ol' Jack, jest like most ol' pranksters, loved to tell uv tricks he'd pulled in the past, an' how things had come to be. As a matter uv fact, he called the past thetaway "the good ol' days." Even today lots o' older folks'll close their eyes, lean back, an' with a smile on their face start talkin'—to their grandkids, who don't understand a word uv it—'bout the "good ol' days."

But you know—an' some uv us oldsters take heart in this—there's some grandkids what'll ask questions, not jest about the meanin' uv the "good ol' days," but 'bout certain things what happened back then. Some o' Ol' Jack's grandkids seemed to be 'bout as curious as he'd been when he's their age, though there was times when the looks on their faces, registered a kind o' jubous (dubious) attitude about the veracity uv the norated account.

One uv his grandkids, by the name uv Cleve, suspected thet there mighta been a connection between Ol' Granddaddy Jack an' the name o' Jack Frost. When asked to 'splain it, Ol' Jack jest said thet Jack Frost was named fer *him*—or after him, whichever seems to make most sense. But he wouldn't lay claim to hit his own self. Hit was Tom, his older brother, what made out Jack Frost got its name from one uv Jack's shenanigans.

You see, what'd happened was thet one Halloween, Jack, when still a young'un, had gone over to Jill's house to skeer her an' her little brother. So he fixed hisself a bucket uv whitewarsh an' got hisself a turkey wing with the feathers still on it, an' while all o' Jill's family was asettin' in front uv the fire, Jack snuck up under the winder. He stuck them turkey feathers into the bucket uv whitewarsh, then scraped 'em acrost the winder, makin' little scratchin' sounds, but leavin' a streakedy lacy patch uv whitenin' on the winderglass.

Jill's little brother, Otis, started whimperin', thinkin' hit was a sure 'nuff Halloween haint, but when Jill went over to the windersill, she said, "Oh, hit ain't nothin' atall. Hit's jest Jack ascratchin' on the winder with a turkey wing."

The very next night when thar was real frost on the winder, Otis piped right up an' said, "Oh, you cain't fool me no more. Thet's jest Jack's frost."

After thet Jack Frost was given credit fer any frosty markin's on winders or punkins or whatever. But, accordin' to Tom, Jack was to blame fer Jack Frost gettin' thet name.

Ol' Jack even tried to take credit fer President Jackson's last name—*Jack's son*— but his grandkids was way ahead uv him on thet one. They knew thet President Jackson had come from a long line uv family Jacksons, so hit musta been another Jack a long time ago, what had a son who went by the name *Jack's son*.

Now, one uv the things Ol' Jack did like to tell about—in order to skeer the chil'ren was about the snakes when he was jest a boy. He was a real expert on tellin' 'bout snakes; one was a milk snake, what'd milk the cow dry, iffen you wadn't careful to keep hit skeered away.

O' course ever'body knowed thet wherever you'd put a rope down, a snake wouldn't crawl over hit. So you'd jest put a rope circle on the ground roun' yore cow to keep her from gettin' milked by a milk snake. But most o' the time—particularly in the daytime when the cows would be grazin' an' all—you couldn't keep 'em inside a rope circle, so you'd run the risk uv not havin' no milk at the next milkin' time.

One o' his favorite snakes was the hoop snake, what'd put hit's tail in his mouth an' roll after you, 'til he'd ketch up with you an' unquile jest afore he flung hisslf back'ards twarge you to gig you with thet pizinous tail.

In fact, accordin' to Ol' Jack, he come upon a bunch o' snakes afightin'. At first he couldn't make out what kinda snakes they was, but then he reckanized 'em. The mortal enemy uv the hoop snake was the mottled, flathead, corkscrew snake. An' thet big mess o' snakes was five hoop snakes an' one mottled, flathead, corkscrew snake. While he was watchin' the battle they killed each other right there in front uv him.

So he got 'em untangled an' cut off the tail uv one hoopsnake, what had his tail in the mouth uv another hoop snake but what was choked to death by the corkscrew snake.

Knowin' 'bout puttin' a horsehair in stump water to turn hit into a snake, Ol' Jack sez, "I'll jest see if I can turn thet 'xperiment back'ards an' put them dead snakes into some swamp water." So, you see, thet's what he done, an' turned them cussed snakes into a fine walkin' stick.

The reason they was five hoop snakes was thet they'd get together, puttin' their tails in each others' mouths. An' thetway

TRICKSTER JACK

they'd make a whole heap bigger hoop an' roll a whole lot faster. Them snakes what would gather together like thet was called "hoopie-groupies."

Ol' Jack loved to tell uv the time a hoop snake nearly got him, but jest as the spear end of thet blamed snake was 'bout to get him when he was standin' next to a young apple tree, he stepped to one side, an' thet straightened-out hoop snake burrowed hisself 'most halfway into thet little tree.

The way Ol' Jack told hit was thet he stood there in sheer amazement as the power o' thet pizinous tail invigorated thet young saplin' uv a apple tree, an' hit took to growin' right then an' there. An' while Ol' Jack—o' course he was young Jack when this happened—was jest astandin' there, hit blossomed, then leafed out, an' apples commenced agrowin, 'til they all got all the way plum ripe.

O' course, accordin' to Ol' Jack, he wouldn't eat none of 'em or take 'em home 'cause he was smart enough to know they was filled with all thet pizen from the hoop snake.

Right then, Ol' Jack would stop hisself to give a little hist'ry lesson to the chil'ren what was listenin'. He'd say, "*Now you know where the mean ol' queen got thet pizinous apple what she give to Sleepin' Beauty to make her sleep fer a hundred years.*" An' the chil'ren did know the Sleepin' Beauty story what Ol' Jack had already made up fer them some time afore, an' they thought thet thet was a logical explanation uv the pizinous apple.

As much as Ol' Jack took delight in tellin' them outlandish stories (what he'd begun to believe his own self), one uv the biggest stories what happened to him wadn't made up atall, an' hit wadn't somethin' he done but what his grandkids done to him—kinda unthoughtedly, so to speak. Actually, they nearly done him in.

You see, hit was like this. Ol' Jack, ever' spring 'bout Easter

Ol' Jack's Indoor-Outhouse

time, he'd figger hit was time fer his annual personal spring cleanin'. Thet's roun' the same time the womenfolk would clean the houses by scourin' all the floors an' walls, gettin' the winter residue outta the pots an' pans an' warshin' an' airin' out all the bedclothes. Thet was also the time fer muckin' out all the barn stalls.

This'd be jest at the right time fer ramps to come up in some uv the low places in the woods. Now, ramps is like what thet Shakespeare writer feller over yonder would call *rampions*. But in the mountains where Jack was from, they was jest called ramps. They was a kind o' wild garlic or leek an' smelled to high heaven. When Jack was younger, he'd bring a mess uv 'em to school, an' the teacher'd have to call school off 'cause uv the stench.

But ramps was better than castor oil fer yore annual constitutional internal ablution.

Now this particular time, what I'm atellin' you 'bout, was the same time they had put indoor plumbin' in the house where Ol' Jack was alivin'... much to his dismay an' objections. He said, "Hit don't seem right now to build a outhouse inside the livin' an' eatin' house. Hit's downright onnatcheral."

Ol' Jack was right proud uv the outhouse he had, what'd been built by the WPA. Hit had German-sidin' plankin' what was painted white—an' I don't mean the ol'-time whitewarshin'—it was really the only white paint on the whole place. But now, the floor an' the seat was genu-wine cement with a lid with a little screen winder to keep the blowfies out. Boy, hit was fancy.

The guvmint built these upgrade outhouses to improve the health conditions in the mountains an' also to give those WPA men somethin' to do. A'course Ol' Jack already had a nice outhouse with a little half-moon decoration. Hit was even a two-holer, an' the new ce-ment one was jest a one-holer.

TRICKSTER JACK

Even after the indoor-outhouse got installed, Ol' Jack'd still use the outdoor-outhouse, unless hit was rainin' or real cold, then he'd 'preciate the convenience. His grandkids thought hit was 'bout time fer Ol' Jack to modernize with the times, so they figgered, all on their own, to get shed uv the ol' outhouse but not tell their Granpap Jack 'bout hit 'til hit was done.

They knowed hit was gonna be a whole lot harder than gettin' rid uv the ol' two-holer outhouse what they'd jest pushed down the hill an' burned. But now this ce-ment-base outhouse was a entirely new challenge.

One o' the boys'd been workin' in the mines an' knew how to use dynamite, so he brung home four sticks to use on the outhouse. They started early one mornin' while Ol' Jack was still asleep…He didn't get up as early uv a mornin' as he usta. They figgered if they'd put one stick uv dynamite under each corner uv the ce-ment pad, hit'd do the job fer sure. So thet's what they done an' then wired thet to a little trigger roun' the corner uv the barn where they wouldn't get hit by none uv the shrapnel.

By the time they was all set to go, Ol' Jack had woke up an' was headed twarge the outdoor-outhouse, unbeknownst to anybody—even them what was preparin' the dynamite trigger. Hit was his spring-cleanin' time, an' the night afore he'd et a big supper uv cornbread, fried taters, a bowl uv pinto beans, an' a whole big mess uv ramps.

Well, boys, don't you know 'bout the time Ol' Jack had sat down, the boys roun' the corner uv the barn was all set to blast 'er off—to the moon, so to speak. They let the littlest boy count fer the countdown, 'cause he'd already started learnin' to count to school.

They even asked him to count back'ards; "Ten…nine…eight…seven…six…five…four…three…two…one…"

Ol' Jack's Indoor-Outhouse

The trigger man yelled, "Let 'er rip!"

An' jest as the KA-BOOM sounded the boys all peered roun' the barn an' seen thet outhouse raise right straight up. Right then the front door uv the outhouse flung open where they could see Ol' Jack asettin' on the throne with his hat floatin' up twarge the roof, his hair standin' straight up, an' his eyes bulgin' out like a granddaddy bullfrog.

The boys'd thought they'd done in their grandpap.

The whole flyin' contraption hovered there fer awhile, then wafted over 'bout fifty feet twarge the barn an' landed jest as all the walls fell outards.

There sat Ol' Jack right in the middle uv the barnyard on the ce-ment throne with his overhauls down roun' his ankles.

He looked at the boys an' pronounced, "Hit was a bless-ed thing!"

(Now I've gotta interrupt myself right here an' explain thet in the mountains, to say "bless-ed thing," hit don't necessarily mean godly or religious-like. Hit mainly jest means "fortunate.")

So he said hit agin. "Hit sure was a bless-ed thing!"

The oldest grandson, Robert, ventured to ask, "What was a bless-ed thing, Papaw Jack?"

"Hit sure was a bless-ed thing I didn't use the indoor-outhouse or the whole house hitself would be gone by now."

I don't think Ol' Jack ever did take to likin' to use thet indoor-outhouse, an' he 'llowed as how spring cleanin' was never the same after thet.

The Jack Game

To play the *Jack game* the players decide to work singly or in teams (two or more), depending on the number of players.

An aphorism, selected by the referee(s), such as *shake a leg* or *saved by the bell*, is assigned to the players. Each person or team is to write a short imaginative narrative of how Jack and/or his brothers came up with that saying. A specific amount of time is announced by the referee(s).

When all players reconvene, each narrative is read, and the winner is chosen either by the referee(s) or voted on by the whole group.

Instead of an aphorism or proverb, an interesting English word, such as *madcap* or *gooseflesh*, may be used to imagine how it would have been originally invented by Jack.

It may be more challenging to explore stories of how Jack first used really difficult English words, such as *obfuscate* or *peripatetic*.

A further variation could be to use a nursery rhyme, such as "Hickory, Dickory, Dock" or "Little Miss Muffet." What circumstances would impel Jack to make up these rhymes or close approximations of them? As you can tell from my Jack stories, some of the sayings and rhymes made up by or about Jack may have been changed later by teachers or other grown-ups.

The purpose of the game is to study neither history nor English but to open the imagination of the player to the sheer enjoyment of playing with language. After all, that's what Shakespeare was doing, which inspired even the illiterate groundlings to watch and listen to *Hamlet* for three hours without even a bench on which to sit.

To listen to these stories in Reid's own voice, you may order CDs from www.jbsproductions.com.